SPACE SHARKS

ALAN SPENCER

SPACE SHARKS

ISBN: 978-1-925342-48-2

SUPER SUCK 3000

The beach was cleared of citizens to allow over ninety semi-trucks to pump water from the Gulf of Mexico. Otis Spooner was one of the many workers hired by Globo Corps to transport the precious resource to the Lyndon B. Johnson Space Center. *God knows why the space center needed hundreds of thousands of gallons of water*, Otis thought. He didn't care. As long as Globo Corps was signing his paychecks, they could ask for anything their mega-rich conglomerate asses wanted.

Otis positioned the sucker tube twelve feet out from the shoreline. While steadying it into the water, he kept hearing odd sounds over the motor's mean churn. Things were banging against the walls of the tube on the way up.

Big heavy things.

Definitely not water.

Suck.

Phuuuuuuump!

Suck.

Phuuuuuuump!

Otis didn't worry about it. The engine worked with so much pressure and power, it could unclog any mess. *But the pipes were sure sucking up something heavy*, Otis thought. It could've been trash, parts of wrecked boats, or even the local aquatic life.

No matter. His instructions were simply to fill the rig's reservoir with water. That was it. Globo had a hard on for water, and when the richest juggernaut in the universe wanted something, they got it ASAP.

Phuuuuuuump!

Phuuuuuuump!

Phuuuuuuump!
Phuuuuuuump!

"How many times is that going to happen? Seriously."

Otis worried if he would *somehow* get into trouble for sucking up more than just water. Orders were orders, but if the shit went down, he didn't want his head on the chopping block. Globo Corps didn't mess around when it came to firing people.

Otis called the site manager, Jim Coogan, on his cell phone.

Jim was more than annoyed by the call.

"Yeah, Spooner? I'm very busy. You get your dick stuck in that thing again? You want someone to help you get it out before it gets ripped off?"

"Um, no, not that, sir," Otis said, fumbling over his words. "I keep sucking up objects into the tank. I'm worried it might break the machine."

"*And?*"

"And, I mean, well, you know, I'm just saying—is this going to be a problem? What if there's something that doesn't belong in the tanks when it reaches its destination? I don't want my butt chewed off. Know what I mean? It's been chewed off over less."

Otis wondered if every other pump operator was dialing in the same question to Coogan.

Jim's gruff was answer enough.

"Just get it done, Spooner. This is a time sensitive project. You let the bozos down at Globo Corps' main office worry about what *else* we suck up. Your job is to fill your rig up with water, and get it down to Houston. How difficult is that? We weren't told to filter the water. That's some other asshole's problem. So suck to your heart's content, and don't call me again unless you have a *real* problem."

Otis swallowed hard. "Thanks, sir."

Fuck you, Coogan. You always got that look about you like someone smeared a line of shit under your nose. That damn sneer. I could cut it from your face, and there'd still be some attitude showing.

Otis kept pumping water, and indulging in a few rants of colorful cussing.

Every few minutes, he'd heard the inevitable: *Phuuuuuuump!*

If Jim Coogan didn't care that the water was harboring random things, and if Globo Corps wasn't sweating it, then Otis Spooner of all people wouldn't give a wet fart about it.

Nobody would know that a wide variety of sharks had snuck into the payload until it was much too late. Soon, few would be alive to learn about the error anyway.

PART ONE: END OF THE PLANET

WE'RE GOING TO BURN

Ram Rogan was jolted awake by the rush of broken glass and the colorful burst of hot flames blasting into his bedroom. His curtains were nothing but fluttering particles of ash by the time his eyes sprang open. The walls were being chewed through by hot flames. Everywhere, fire!

The recent warnings in the news were correct. The world would soon be on fire, and absolutely nothing could quell the flames. The pollution crisis had reached critical mass. The atmosphere had turned toxic. The earth had a reset button, and it had been pressed hard. Temperatures beneath the earth's crusts were steadily rising. Scholars and naturalists alike predicted the earth would turn against its inhabitants anytime now. Nobody knew it would be an overnight transition from safe to fiery abyss.

We still had time, every scientist proclaimed. Years, decades maybe, every mode of media had promised.

They were lies.

The earth had no time left, and everybody was going to burn.

Ram wasn't going to let himself die without a fight. The earth had made its choice, and now he had choices of his own to make.

By the time he put his shoes on and made a dash for the living room, the bedroom was reduced to a fiery death inferno. His Samoan butt retreated to the front door for escape.

All the living room windows suddenly burst. Jet-burner streams of fire bathed his domicile. His collection of NFL trophies as the quarterback of the St. Louis Rams were melting into something morbid looking. Everything was burning bright. He could hear screams throughout the building as people were being cooked alive. The reek of scorched flesh tainted the air. Ram coughed against the acrid, black smoke that filled his lungs.

Nobody was going to make it out alive. Still, Ram had to try and survive. His basic human instincts kicked into serious overdrive.

Roast or run.

Ram chose run.

He plowed into the hallway with flames licking at his back. The long length of doors into other apartments were actively ablaze. Smoke was pouring through the cracks, reducing visibility. Fires were downgrading the walls into kindling. Explosions, like bursting gas lines, rocked the property outside. Things didn't appear to be safe inside or outside.

Everywhere, death.

Two-thirds of the apartment structure erupted as if a C-4 bomb had been triggered. The wall nearest Ram went up into torn up smithereens. Ram back-pedaled in the other direction. There was the only way left to go, and that was towards the emergency stairs.

Before he could open that door, it was thrown open for him.

Out stumbled the building's superintendent.

Carlos Martinez's face was like melting pizza. Flesh was popping and oozing in liquid mudslides of skin. It wasn't from the fire. His skin was sizzling and melting from something...*else.*

Carlos' screams were blood-curdling. He pleaded to Ram in a terrible shrill, "It's raining acid! Don't go outside! God help us! Death is everywhere!"

Carlos pressed a .45 pistol to his skull. His hand was melting into the gun's handle before he pulled the trigger.

Ram knew what was about to go down. "No, don't do it!"

Carlos put a bullet between his eyes.

Ram staggered two steps away from the super's corpse. He didn't have many choices now. The hallway behind him was entirely engulfed in flames.

No go.

The emergency stairs would be like taking a step into hell's furnace. Ram could vaguely make out the mottled black bodies thrashing in the incendiary colors as they slowly burned to death on the stairs.

Check that off the list.

Outside, if Carlos was right—and judging by his skin, Carlos was right on the money!—would be an acid rain shower waiting for him. If Ram enjoyed his skin, he wouldn't dare go outside.

From top to bottom, the fourteen story apartment building was attacked by new explosions. The force of one BOOM threw Ram against the big bay window near the emergency exit. His two-hundred and thirty pound bulk easily broke through the glass. He plummeted three stories down and landed in the deep end of the apartment complex's pool. Other people had had the idea of jumping into the pool for safety earlier. Some made it down successfully, while others had struck the pavement and broke their bodies. The lucky ones died on impact. The unlucky ones writhed in agony.

The rain pelting down onto the city was melting trees, setting grass on fire, and acting as liquid bullets as they struck hapless victims as they ran for their miserable lives. Some drops acted as napalm; one drop dissolved every ounce of flesh and sucked every fluid dry from the human body in seconds. Others spontaneously combusted. Some would go off like bizarre fireworks. Their heads would explode and unleash sprays of flames and boiling blood from the neck. Arms and legs would blast off, releasing unreal fountains of fire.

Ram stayed under the pool's surface. The city was rocked by what sounded like missile attacks. Ambulances and police sirens wailed. Choppers flew across the sky only to be exploded by the elements. Human suffering echoed from every cardinal direction.

Ram was losing air. He could hear others gasp and struggle to decide whether to return to the surface for air and risk death, or to drown and forget it all.

He had his eyes open when the bottom of the pool came undone. They were sitting on top of a volcano, the way the flames exploded through the concrete and sent them airborne. Once he reached about six feet up, he was delivered back down to the ground. When he hit the grass, Ram wasn't sure where he'd been relocated. He could only collect himself up off of the ground, shake his possibly concussed head, avoid the flames around him, and see everything be eaten by reds, yellows, and oranges.

He was standing underneath a burning tree now. He was near his apartment building at the edge of a dog park. The cityscape looked to have been bombed by incendiary missiles. Some in the streets who'd been kicked out of buildings by the raging flames stood with wide open arms as the acid rain melted their skin from top to bottom. They were plastic figurines in a microwave set too high. They realized the fight was futile. Death would be a blessing. And they accepted that blessing.

Ram couldn't process such decisions. Who wanted to think of suicide as the better option? Certainly not him. The things he'd been through in one lifetime were far worse than any scorching hot death kiss.

A hand covered in melting sores and popping flesh covered Ram up with a large silver blanket. Underneath that silver blanket stood a woman in her mid-thirties. She was terrified and covered in gray soot. Ram didn't process the woman so much. He focused more on the pitiful man who was dying from serious burns.

Half the man's face was edging off of his bones and staining his shirt in greasy smears. One hand clutched Ram by the collar of his shirt, and the other hung limp at his side, having lost all of its skin.

The voice was pure agony. "Listen to me. Keep your ears open, big man. I'm as good as dead. It's simple, if you want to live. You stay under this blanket, and it'll keep you safe from the acid rain. This doesn't come free, pal. Here's the deal. You get to live, if you swear to me you'll see my daughter to safety. *See her into the new world.*"

"But how, I—"

"Listen!"

The man's waxy lips dripped down his chin to reveal bared teeth. "Promise me you'll see her to safety. Gaby's my daughter. Promise me you'll look after her, even after the world is gone."

The man's good hand slapped a plastic wristwatch with a big box at the top onto Ram's wrist. There was no face for a clock. A green dot blinked on the box in the bottom corner. The watch's purpose was unclear.

"They're looking for us right now. This is a tracking device. Stay under the blanket. Don't move. They'll pick you up soon.

Now promise me you'll honor your end of the bargain. See Gaby to safety."

"I PROMISE! Now tell me what this is all about. Who are you?"

"No time. Honor this deal. Do it for a dead man."

The man turned away from his daughter, and hobbled out from underneath the safety of the silver blanket.

"I love you, Gaby. I pray you get to live in the new world. It's all I ever wanted for you. I'm sorry it had to end this way. The things I knew. The things *they* kept from the world. Many innocent people died. Maybe they didn't have to. Forgive me! I made things worse. I helped them."

"Dad, no!"

Ram had the instinct to hold Gaby back with one arm. She was a frail thing, and he easily kept her in place. When her father was doused in acid rain, he instantly melted down to bones. Soon after that, the man was simply vapor drifting across a scorched landscape.

Ram wasn't sure how to console Gaby. "Don't look. He's gone. I'm sorry."

Gaby put her face into Ram's chest and sobbed.

The gray plastic watch on his wrist suddenly beeped. The green light turned solid. Ram heard a rush of air from above. What touched down was a giant steel box with twin thruster engines burning hot. He thought of a spacecraft from the future the size of two mini-vans combined. The acid rain and fire did nothing to harm the exterior. From below the hovercraft vehicle, a step ladder was dropped down to their position.

From the hovercraft, a voice spoke through an intercom.

"*Climb up to safety. Time is limited. You must hurry.*"

Ram absorbed a new series of screams from nearby, as he did the sights of buildings toppling over and being consumed by raging fire. This was his only chance to live. Whatever promise he'd made to the dead man, Ram decided to honor it.

"Get onto my back, Gaby."

Gaby did so without question. Ram climbed up each rung of the rope ladder. When he reached the bottom of the vehicle, a slot underneath the hovercraft opened. Rescue workers reached out to help the two of them up into the main cab. Once inside, they were seated in a small area with six other persons who were shaken up and covered in grit and ash.

The two rescue workers wore black helmets with blue tinted faceplates. The two removed Ram's and Gaby's watches. Underneath the thick box was a barcode. The rescue workers scanned the codes.

One of the workers announced, "Gaby Reigns and General Reigns. That completes the list. Everybody is picked up. Now let's get a move on to base, before everything goes to hell. There's only one way off this planet, and it's about to leave in thirty minutes."

ON THE WAY TO SAFETY

This wasn't a time to talk.

This was the time to recover.

Everybody was silent in the main cab. Those inside the hovercraft watched the world come undone through the thick plated glass. The view was horrible. The city of Houston was literally engulfed in flames. The skies were spewing acid rain that pelted the city and turned everything into a simmering death broth. Lightning branches caused sonic boom blasts. Those branches ruined skyscrapers, destroyed cityscapes, and treated the city of Houston like a battlefield. They were high up enough that they couldn't see individual people be melted down. Ram thanked God for that small favor.

He thought back to how the man scanning their watches called Ram "General Reigns". If they knew his real identity, would they kick him off of this ride? He made a promise to a man in the throws of death. See Gaby to safety.

Ram would do just that.

He wouldn't chance his life asking risky questions.

Concerns piled up in Ram's mind. How could this hovercraft survive the acid rain and fire? Why were people wearing the plastic watches saved, and the others without them were left to die? And where the hell were they going? The earth was cooked.

Gaby's death-pale face remained still. Tears had dried around her eyes. Her straight blonde hair was covered in ashes. She wouldn't meet Ram's stare. If he could get any information out of her, it would help him figure these things out.

She just watched her father melt to death.

She may need more than a minute to cope.

Yeah, and you just watched some sick shit go down too.

There isn't any time to go to pieces.

Ram was about to ask somebody sitting in the seats where they were going when one of the two rescuers spoke up.

"We're about to land. Prepare yourselves. Once we land, we need to move, and move fast. We're slightly behind schedule. Don't be alarmed. We only ask you do as we say, and ask the questions you have later. Anybody who goes against protocol will be left behind. Trust me; you don't want to be left behind."

Ram's gut was telling him something was very wrong about this situation. Why weren't others rescued? There had to be others out there who were alive and facing peril.

The sight below stole Ram away from his thoughts. He couldn't peel his eyes from the shocking thing. The hovercraft was lowering down towards the Lyndon B. Johnson Space Center.

What was left of it.

Most of it was burning bright and collapsing. The only thing that didn't burn was the giant globe of steel. The huge black ball was standing topside on a helipad. The bottom of the ball had four giant rocket thrusters. Ram imagined a space hamster ball on steroids. He guessed it could fit thousands of people inside, easily. The steel could take on fire and acid rain without sustaining any damage.

The pilot up front announced, "Approaching *The Redeemer.* Hold tight, folks. We're almost to safety. *Keep your eyes set to the future.*"

The hovercraft fast-approached *The Redeemer.* A slot opened on the side of the giant ship, and they flew inside. After traveling in a dark tunnel, a light appeared up ahead. A small docking station materialized.

Once they landed, Ram would learn the truth about *The Redeemer*, and those specially chosen to board the vessel.

THE REDEEMER

The landing pad stretched the length of an airplane hanger. Hovercrafts, the same ones that delivered them inside the giant globe, were lined up in a side-by-side formation. Almost a hundred of the crafts were being unloaded of persons. Shaken up survivors were being led by the men in black helmets and blue visors. The pilots and crew wore white jumpsuits covered in thick armor. Ram noticed they had holsters equipped with taser guns and wooden batons.

A message repeated over the intercom.

"STEP INTO LINE ONE IN FRONT OF THE OTHER. ABSOLUTELY NO TALKING. ALL YOUR QUESTIONS WILL BE ANSWERED VERY SOON. IF YOU HAVE ANY MEDICAL NEEDS, PLEASE RAISE YOUR HANDS. ONE OF OUR ASSISTANTS WILL BE RIGHT WITH YOU. STAY CALM. YOU ARE SAFE. YOU ARE ON THE REDEEMER."

A crewperson urged Gaby into the forming line. Ram forced his way forward so he was right behind her. Gaby didn't want anything to do with him. She was deathly pale and visibly shivering. He hoped she would snap out of it soon so they could talk.

Ram didn't push her with questions. If he forced explanations, he would only be denied. Timing was everything. The best plan he had was to keep her in his line of sight, and then let her come to him.

Ram couldn't believe what had happened. The city of Houston had melted. Who knew how much of the earth remained uncooked? Environmental concerns were at the forefront of politics and news lately. Smog, acid rain, and global warming were hot topics, but these were supposed to be concerns to worry about centuries from now, not in the present tense. Whoever owned this mega craft and arranged for people with the wristwatches to be picked up amidst the chaos knew something the rest of the people didn't.

Questions, questions, questions, and Ram had no way to answer them.

He followed the intercom's commands. He walked calmly behind Gaby. They left the landing area and entered a single narrow hallway. The tight chambers smelled of burnt clothing, sweat, and echoed with the subtle sound of crying.

The hallway emptied out into a larger room. He compared it to a giant movie theatre, minus the seating. Everybody stood in front of a giant screen. Ten minutes passed before the lights finally dimmed and an image appeared on the screen.

A symbol with a cartoon picture of Earth was shown, and then the Earth turned the color of gold. Beneath the symbol it read: **Globo Corps**. A woman's voice spoke through the state-of-the-art sound system and announced, "*Globo Corps. Eyes set to the future.*"

Ram wasn't sure why his stomach did a flip. He felt like an interloper. That general who melted near his apartment was supposed to be standing here with his daughter, not him.

Before he could worry anymore, the presentation began.

An older scientist dressed in a lab coat with graying hair combed back into a ponytail stood in front of a giant graphic of blue prints and started talking.

"Hello, my name is Dr. Dean Fleming. You each have been selected to be delivered to Second Earth on our vessel, *The Redeemer*. Through Globo Corps' selection process, you have been specially chosen by lottery, class, contribution to society, and special vocations and skills. You will be needed to ensure what happened on Earth does not happen on Second Earth. We must ensure the future of the human race by learning from our previous mistakes. Globo Corps has brought you all here to do just that."

Dr. Dean Fleming disappeared. The screen showed a live feed via space satellite. The shot was a wide-panning view of Earth.

Across every inch of land, earth was in flames. Parts of the earth imploded, sunk into itself, and was replaced by a red hot mass of liquid like magma. The planet resembled the sun, how it seethed heat and boiled.

The scientist continued to narrate:

"Please, don't let this alarm you. *The Redeemer* has already taken off and left the danger zone. We are safe. Yes, I'm afraid the earth is going to explode in approximately seven minutes and thirty seconds. Globo Corps has seen this coming for years. Before we could build enough vessels to save all humans from this catastrophe, our time had run out. This is the best we could do under time, budget, and technological constraints.

"Why the earth has seemingly heated up and destroyed itself is a bit of mystery. Sure, pollution and global warming are suspects, but the best hypothesis, my hypothesis, is that the earth was simply on a timer. It's time has come and gone. Now it's time for a new world. There was nothing anybody could do to stop this inevitable crisis. We need to take this golden opportunity to start over and really run with it. It's a tragedy so much life has been lost. That's why we must cherish this gift and embrace this new opportunity to tread into the future that is much smarter, and kinder, to the environment."

Dr. Fleming stood in front of a graphic of the solar system. The planets shifted around, and it stopped on a distant blue speck far out in the galaxy.

"Twenty years ago, Globo Corps, through private research, happened upon a planet much like Earth. The conditions there can sustain human life. We can grow crops, build housing, and secure the future of humanity. Globo Corps decided to keep this a secret while we conducted research, built housing, and had people live on the planet to prove its sustainability over a period of time."

The camera closed in on Dr. Fleming's gaunt face.

The man lived and breathed insane science.

"I know this is so much to take in at once, so I'll skip to the most important stuff: how this affects you. We want this ride to be a relaxed adventure. *The Redeemer* has been built as a fun ship, as much as a military vessel. That means open bars, dancing, partying, and letting it all go. So enjoy what Globo Corps has provided you. I wish you safe travels. As the surviving members of Earth, we have a great responsibility to secure the future of humanity. We must carry the torch proudly."

The film ended.

The lights were turned back on.

Everybody stared at the screen as if they expected more information to come. The answers provided weren't satisfactory. The horror of Earth being gone had yet to sink in, and having this new information forced upon them was too much to ingest, or that was Ram's take. Saying the room overflowed with nervous energy would be an understatement.

That's why Ram didn't expect the boisterous fat man dressed in a black business suit from behind him to declare, "It's Ram Rogan! I'll be damned. It's really you. The man. The legend. I thought this day couldn't get any crazier. Ram Rogan. Best damn quarterback the St. Louis Rams ever had. Forget Tom Brady, or Joe Namath, and those other assholes. You throw a pigskin with that laser rocket arm like no other. You got a hand cannon. Mega launcher, more like it. Man, the year you won the Super Bowl, you became a hero. That was so awesome. You made America's heart skip a beat. I'm a big fan of yours. *Huge* fan."

Ram remembered that Super Bowl game. It was the last of his career. Ram was known to throw a football so hard that he broke his wide receivers' fingers. The number of touchdowns, rushing yards, and games he won meant nothing up against one statistic.

One religious terrorist killed.

Ram took out Jake Lazar. Jake was the leader of the religious movement called "Red Salvation". This group aimed to steer the world back into God's grace by any means necessary, including murdering, bombing, and executing public figures in public places to get their message across. They were the first American religious cult group in years to take the forefront of the news and gain attention on such a mainstream level.

Jack Lazar chose to sneak into the end zone of Ram's final game with enough explosives attached to his body to take out the entire stadium. Before Jake could finish his anti-American rant,

Ram chucked a Hail Mary pass from fifty yards out that struck Jack Lazar in the face so hard, it shattered the bones of his nose and shoved those shards into his brain and instantly killed him.

Ram Rogan saved the day, and instantly became a national hero. Ram enjoyed the notoriety, the endorsements, the commercial time, the sex, the drugs, the fame, but the group Red Salvation had plans for Ram and his family. It cost him so much later on down the line, and to think about the big game delivered a fresh sense of dread into this already terrible situation.

Dealing with this fan who picked him out of a crowd of weary survivors wasn't something Ram was ready to deal with, so he acknowledged that yes, he was in fact Ram Rogan. *The* Ram Rogan.

"I'm Ernie Pine." Ernie shook Ram's hand vigorously. "It's an honor. Purely an honor."

Before Ram could attempt to dodge the questions, a group of men in the white suits and heavy armor with head gear charged in at Ram. Before Ram could question why they were coming after him, he was tasered. Electricity surged into his body.

Ram dropped to his knees and unleashed a roar of agony. The electricity under his skin paralyzed him. Two more taser guns joined in, and he was blasted with such an electric charge, Ram blanked out. The last thing he saw was Gaby's horrified face, and the panicked crowd recoil from the scene.

PART TWO: ALL SYSTEMS ARE GO—MAYBE

POWER STATION

"I had to suck the biggest dick to get this job."

"At least you only had to suck one. I had a whole room of dicks to deal with, and believe me, not a single person on Globo Corp's committee had a problem getting it up."

"Hey, I'm not complaining. You shouldn't either. I'm grateful to be alive. Our families got on board this one-way ship free and clear."

"Lucky is not strong enough a word, buddy. Thousands applied for our positions and got turned down flat."

"Yeah, and they're probably vapor floating in deep space by now."

"Globo Corp didn't make it easy to get that golden ticket onto the *Redeemer*."

"Yeah. We earned it. Now we got a job to do. If we complete the task, we'll be set for life. We shouldn't complain. Ever."

Marty "Mooch" Mitchell and Joslin Davis sat in chairs side-by side in front of a control panel that controlled the ship's power supply. Mooch and Joslin were one of very few who understood *The Redeemer*'s special source of fuel. The ship didn't run on rocket fuel. The ship's energy solely relied on what functioned beyond the large Plexiglas pane above the control panels. That special room was almost as tall and wide as the ship itself. The rooms, the balconies, and common areas were built around this special area: the core.

The core itself was twenty stories tall. Tubes made of plastic and thick as sewer channels were placed here. Mooch would compare the sight to a person's large intestine, how the tubes piled one-on-top of other. The fluid inside the so-called "intestinal track engine" was a bright pink substance.

Dr. Fleming had invented a super fluid that acted as fuel, coolant, and a source of energy to propel the *Redeemer* to Second Earth. Fleming himself dubbed the fuel "Hydrolyne". The actual contents of the substance were unknown to anyone besides the good doctor, and those at the very top of Globo Corps' corporate ladder. To watch the pink move through the clear plastic was really like looking at a giant's large intestine. The middle of the ship truly served as the "guts" of the vessel.

Dr. Fleming claimed as long as the "Hydrolyne" was immersed in water, the fluid would remain in perpetual motion. This motion propelled the engines cleanly and safely.

Mooch considered the ship's energy source a bunch of egghead nonsense. He had one concern on his mind during his time in the power supply room, and he voiced it.

"You think what those idiots at Globo Corps sucked up out of the ocean along with that water could cause a problem?"

Joslin shook her know-it-all head. "Mooch, you worry too much. The filters will chop up any debris. All problems have been anticipated. We got this."

Mooch accessed an internal camera inside the plastic tube near the middle of the guts. Through the video feed, they viewed the fast flowing pink water.

Joslin huffed. "*Wow*, it's pink stuff. Big deal. Why are we wasting time on this?"

Mooch pointed at the screen. "There! You see it?"

"Yeah, so what?"

"That was a hammerhead shark. It's alive. After being in there for nearly three weeks. How can that be?"

Joslin laughed. "It's not getting out. So what? Who cares?"

"How come the filters haven't destroyed it?"

"Somehow it bypassed the filters. They're not getting out, the ship's on course, the engine's are running correctly, the pressure gauges indicate nothing to be concerned about, so why are you worrying?"

"Three weeks swimming in that pink stuff, you'd think a shark would be dead by now."

Joslin patted Moose on the shoulder. "Yeah, I think sharks can live awhile without eating. But three weeks sure is a long time to go without a meal. I bet they're hungry. And probably pissed off."

Mooch agreed with the last statement. "I've seen about a hundred sharks swim in the guts of the ship. Amazing how they've survived this long. I still think—"

"Stop worrying. They won't escape. Take my word for it. Nothing can go wrong as long as we're at the helm. Right?"

Mooch swallowed hard. "Yeah. Sure. Nothing can go wrong."

GABY REIGNS

Gaby Reigns had been escorted to a private room by one of the many guards on *The Redeemer*. The room matched that of a fine hotel. Nice carpeting, hot tub, big screen TV, mini bar, and all the accoutrements of high end comfort. Gaby stood in the bathroom and washed her face, guzzled the water she cupped in her hands from under the faucet, and did her best to gain back her composure.

This moment was right after the man named Ram Rogan was tasered and clubbed into unconsciousness. Ernie Pine reassured her Ram needed to be handled in a special way, because he wasn't invited to be on the ship, no matter what the circumstances.

Gaby hated Ernie Pine. Slime ball snake. He could slither up inside you, mess with your mind, and control you. That's what Ernie Pine did to her father.

She knew Ernie Pine all too well. The bald grease ball met with her father, General Reigns, to discuss important things over high end scotch, higher end cigars, and big business. Government stuff, her father would say. Classified information. Need to know basis. Shut your ears, my sweet daughter, type stuff.

Bitterness swelled in her core and flowed out of her eyes in the form of bitter hot tears. Gaby knew little of what her father did in the military. General Reigns worked in Iraq. He trained troops. He dealt with terrorist threats. He met with the president many times to discuss war strategies. Her father was on his way up the military food chain. How high did her father go, Gaby often wondered. And now that the world had ended, Gaby had found out something horrible about her father.

This information came to her mere hours ago, when everything started burning on Earth. Before her father could wrap her mother up in that silver blanket and wait for rescue, a window shattered, and she was bathed in fire. Cooked instantly, and thoroughly.

Her mother had confessed one thing to Gaby before that happened.

"...*You can't trust your father anymore. He knew this was going to happen. The fire. The burning. Everybody being in danger. Him and Ernie Pine could've saved many more people. They chose not to. They want to be at the top. They want to rule the new world. They're evil. Your father plans to kill me when we get on the new planet, so he can have all the women he wants. He only loves you, Gaby. Get on that planet, but don't you ever trust that evil man. Your father is no longer the man you once knew.*"

Something wasn't right, that much was clear. Then Ernie Pine treating the stranger, Ram Rogan, like he was a criminal, and taking him away to do Gods knows what with him aroused many suspicions within her.

Her father loved her. Gaby knew this for certain. The problem now, what would Ernie Pine do without his partner? What was the ultimate plan once they arrived on Second Earth?

"...*be bathed in blood, for the lord seeks vengeance upon those who subvert his word. We are not the chosen. We are not the holy. We have been condemned to die. God has demanded the end of humanity, and so it shall be done, by God's hands, and mine.*"

Gaby couldn't see the man speaking in whispers. She only felt the cold knife jammed into her back, right between the shoulder blades. Before it pierced through her heart, a hand twisted her neck to the side, and snapped it with incredible force.

She died instantly.

HE'S SAMOAN!

"You can't be serious? You've risked everything."

"But I am serious. Use your head. People know Ram Rogan's on board. I shouldn't have greeted him like I did, but I had to confirm he was who he was before we engaged him. It was the only way to handle this situation. I'm sorry. I acted impulsively."

"You jumped the gun, Ernie. Now we have to do this the hard way."

Ram Rogan guessed he was laying on a bed, or a cot. Whatever it was, the mattress was hard as a rock. The blow to the back of the skull was a low rumble of ache. He decided not to open his eyes, and instead listen to the two men caught up in a heated discussion.

"Gaby confirmed that General Reigns and his wife are both dead. That means it's up to us to really take control of things. That's a big responsibility. We've worked so hard to procure funds to allow Globo Corps' project to come to fruition. I don't want some washed up football hero to fuck it all up."

"How can he change anything? He's one man."

"He's Samoan! So much planning, and for this to happen? It's bad enough a lot of people who were supposed to be on board didn't make it. This catastrophe was unpredictable. We had it down to the month, but not down to the day. This project was supposed to be re-starting society from scratch.

"We'd have sixty-three percent whites, twenty-eight percent blacks, and nine percent other. Ram will throw it all off. He's Samoan. He'll mate with every pair of female legs in the place, and our population plan will be wrecked. I won't stand for it. This is our chance to do things our way. I'm the president of Globo

Corps for a reason. I know what our people want, and Ram isn't it. This should be a slam dunk, frankly. We don't have billions of people to keep happy anymore. We've got thousands. They'll be so easy to manipulate."

Who the fuck is this guy? So what if I'm Samoan? At least I'm not an asshole. What kind of a spaceship is this?

"Calm down, sir. Ram Rogan won't mate with anyone. I'll make sure of that. I promise you. But we can't outright kill him. People on board have been asking about Ram. They want to see him. He's a celebrity. They want to know if he's okay. I mean, we clubbed his ass good."

"That shit-for-brains lunk head? Why? He's been out of the spotlight for some time now. So he threw a football at some terrorist's face at a Super Bowl and killed him? Whoopee."

"Sir, hear me out. America loved that. That was the highest rated Super Bowl ever. How many people wanted to serve a knuckle sandwich to a real terrorist? And you take Ram, and he used a football to do the job! I mean, Goddamn. You don't get more American than that."

"I'm still not sure where you're going with this, Ernie. You haven't convinced me that we shouldn't perform a lethal injection on this slab of meat and call it a day."

"Let me pitch you this idea," Ernie, the guy Ram remembered in the business suit from earlier, insisted. "Those on board *The Redeemer* have seen Earth implode on itself. They've witnessed their loved ones burned to death. It's not a pleasant sight. The smell of cooked human flesh is seared into my nostrils. It'll take weeks to remove the stink. What I'm saying, sir, is the people here have been served one heck of a shock. They're on a super ship headed to a new planet. It's far-fetched, it's crazy, and you mix that with witnessing mass death, and you got a ship of people who need a familiar face to reassure them all is okay.

"We lost Ben Affleck and Ozzy Osbourne in the fires of Los Angeles. Ram Rogan is the best you got, and your passengers are begging for him. If Ram doesn't reappear, they'll start asking questions. They'll start to distrust us. We can't have that. So we messed up by attacking him. We regroup and recover. What do you say?"

"As long as he doesn't knock up any of the passengers, you can do what you want with the quarterback."

Ernie's voice darkened. "Make no mistake, sir, Ram Rogan didn't make the list. He's not supposed to be here. I haven't forgotten that. Once we touch down on Second Earth, Ram won't leave the ship. An accident will prevent him from joining our society. I'll make it believable."

"Good deal, Ernie. I knew I put you in charge for good reason."

AWAKE

Ram waited for the men to leave before he opened his eyes. When he tried to lift himself out of bed, someone eased him back down. They had just entered the room.

"Easy, Mr. Rogan. Take it slow."

The room wasn't very big. Just large enough for a bed, a sink, and a cabinet full of medical supplies. Ram noticed a nearby trashcan full of torn up gauze, dirty cotton balls, and rags used to clean burn wounds.

Ram paused to behold the nurse in light blue scrubs and jeans. She had curly blonde hair, a muscled body that had seen many days at the gym, and a pair of eyes that extended sympathy and understanding. Ram couldn't avoid her stare, because it was so intoxicating, those soft sea-blue eyes. It was the best thing he'd seen in he didn't know how long. For a moment, he forgot how he was a marked man by Globo Corps.

Ram kept his calm. The two men were gone. Then again, if this woman produced a needle and tried to poke him, Ram would be at the ready to stop her.

"Are you a one woman show?"

"I'm afraid so, Mr. Rogan. I was supposed to have two others as assistants, but they didn't make it here alive. We lost a lot of people that way. Everything happened so fast. Globo Corps predicted a lot of things, but they couldn't predict everything."

"Like me getting on this ship?"

"Yeah. If you're not on the list, they freak out about it."

"I could use a drink. You have anything besides rubbing alcohol in this place?" Ram noticed her nametag read: Buffy King. "Well, Buffy, how about a drink? To Second Earth?"

Buffy realized how he knew her name, and she let out a soft laugh. "How clever, Mr. Rogan. You read my nametag."

"Call me Ram."

"Okay, Ram. Don't tell anybody about my stash."

She removed a bottle of bourbon from the bottom compartment of the cabinet. Buffy used a paper cup from the water cooler and poured a healthy dose for each of them.

"To Second Earth," Buffy proposed.

"To Second Earth." *If I make it there alive.*

Ram drank his, and Buffy finished hers with equal zest.

"A cigarette would go great with this," Buffy sighed. "My husband said I couldn't smoke anymore."

Ram felt around in his pockets. Of all the things that had happened to him since the moment his apartment burned down, there had been a pack in his pants pocket, and the cigarettes inside remained intact. He hadn't opened the package before now.

"Here, keep the pack. I breathed in enough smoke today. I think I want to quit."

"There won't be any cigarettes on Second Earth," Buffy said. She fished out a cigarette by hitting the pack with her palm once. She searched several drawers and located a box of matches. "Smoke if you got 'em. Now I got 'em. David can kiss my ass."

"Who's David?"

"My husband. He died today."

"I'm so sorry."

Buffy enjoyed a tug on her cigarette. Her craving was deep.

"Don't be. He was a major asshole. It's a long, terrible story."

Before Ram could react to her statement, the familiar fat bald man in a suit entered the room. Ernie Pine.

Ernie had an apologetic look about him.

The expression was as genuine as faux leather.

"Ram! You're awake. I am so, so sorry about what transpired earlier. Security heard your name wasn't on the list, and they acted without thinking. Please accept my apologies. I see our nurse here has patched you up in good order."

Ram finally noticed the bandage on the back of his head.

"Yes. She did a wonderful job."

"She's the best and only nurse we got," Ernie said. "Anyway, if we can rise above this unfortunate situation, I have a favor to ask you. I know, *me* asking *you* a favor."

Ram had to play dumb, and play along, so he spoke with careful deliberation.

"You mean you're not mad I'm on board?"

Ernie smiled. He believed the dumb jock would go along with his plan. "Of course not. You're a hero. You saved Gaby's life. Whether you know it or not, Gaby is the daughter of a high-ranking military official. He had a lot to do with the building of *The Redeemer*. We have no reason not to embrace your presence here.

"But back to that favor, Ram. We've got a lot of people who need a morale boost. They've seen hell, frankly. Would you do us the honor of attending a sort of meet and greet? Just talk with people. Try to uplift them. You're a national hero, Ram."

Yeah, I was *a hero. They call it your fifteen minutes. I burned those up in ten. Then I landed on my ass in a pile of shit.*

Whatever, fuck face. I'm watching you.

"I'm a nobody," Ram said, "but if you think they want to see me, I'm happy to do whatever to help out. Despite the mix-up, I'm very fortunate to be on this ship. I don't deserve the honor."

"Sure you do," Buffy said with alarming conviction. "A lot of people who deserved to be here didn't make it. You got here by saving someone's life. You knew nothing about *The Redeemer*, or where it was going. What you did was heroic, and honest."

"Yeah, absolutely, yes, heroic," Ernie butted in. "You're a true American. A saint. A good man. Are you well enough I can give you the quick tour? Then you can meet those on board?"

"I think I'm okay. My head's still ringing a little. I'll get over it. I'm an ex-football player. I'm used to being banged up."

"Check back in with me later," Buffy said. Her blue eyes wouldn't leave him. Was that a come on, or just genuine concern? "I want to look you over one more time."

"That can be arranged," Ernie said, trying to brush her off. "Okay, Ram. Let's get you up and about."

You got it, dick breath. Pull any fast ones, and I'll break you in two.

Ram left the medical infirmary with Ernie and would soon see the rest of *The Redeemer*.

THE GUTS OF THE SHIP

Mooch couldn't stop playing with the video feeds inside the vast network of plastic tubing. Watching the pink substance flow in the tubes was a show in itself. He kept seeing things swimming in the flow, and it was starting to trouble him.

One detail in particular.

There weren't just sharks mixed up in the mess. There were many types of sharks. Bull sharks. Thresher sharks. Blacktip sharks. Great white sharks. Tiger sharks. Lemon sharks. Fine tooth sharks. Hammerhead sharks. Mud sharks. The population of sea life didn't stop there. There was also fish, like salmon, rainbow trout, bass, carp, blue gill, and barracuda. Every once in awhile, a squid, or a sea otter, would also appear.

Joslin started to enjoy the game of spotting living things in the pink tubes. That was until they noticed one disturbing detail about the aquatic life.

Mooch and Joslin reeled at the sights.

They panned in closer on the camera to get a real close view. The digital camera displayed the images on their control panel screens with alarming clarity.

There were many sets of gnarly teeth.

Everything had crazy choppers.

"I've never seen anything like it before," Mooch said. "Sharks have crazy teeth to begin with, but this is insane!"

Joslin agreed. "It's like they have more teeth too, and they're so jagged. That bull shark's got at least two hundred teeth. I mean, how? Good God, they'd rip right through you. Our flesh would be like butter to those things."

Mooch pictured a seesaw with super jacked up steel teeth. They would slice into meat just like a saw, matched with the jaw power of a great white.

"Even the fish have more teeth. A blue gill shouldn't look like a damn barracuda, and a barracuda shouldn't look like a blender from hell. What's happening to them?"

Joslin kept studying the feeds. "It's not just their teeth. They look...stronger."

"Stronger?"

"Their bodies are thicker. I mean, they're ripped. Their skin looks so thick. These sharks are on steroids."

"Wait, wait, wait." Mooch kept disbelieving his eyes. "I've looked in on our fishy friends like three hours ago, and they didn't have crazy ass teeth then. It's like the transformation just occurred. It's impossible, but there it is. And you're right, they do look like they've been taking steroids. Jesus, did you see that crab?"

Joslin started to type out commands on the control panel. "We can't have these creatures getting bigger and bigger. The plastic tubing is thick, so it'd be unlikely they'd escape that way. But if they get too big, the filters won't be able to, well, you know, chop them up."

"That's another thing I don't understand," Mooch said, trying to get a grip on his nerves. "We've chopped up ten tons of trash, debris, and even dogs, cats, and a few dead homeless people. It's like the fish are stronger than the filter's suction, and they're consciously fighting against it."

"I'm turning up the filter's power." Joslin ramped up the suction speed to full blast. "Let's watch what happens. This should take care of them."

At each end of the tubes, engines began to suction the pink water towards the thick steel blades spinning like that of a mega-garbage disposal. Joslin and Mooch watched, hunched over their screens, and hoped their plan worked.

The pink water began to froth and fizz as the tide was pulled in a new direction. Many of the smaller fish and sharks were forced through the filters and out the other side. They were rendered into pureed matter instantly.

But that only accounted for the smallest creatures. The rest were swimming against the tide, and battling to stay in place. The sharks, their bodies rippling with strength and power, remained unaffected. The suction was nothing up against their strength. After ten minutes straight, Joslin decided not to wear the filter engines down. If those broke down, then they'd be in serious trouble.

"Maybe if we monitor them," Mooch said, thinking out loud, "and make sure they don't leave the tubes, everything will be okay? The sharks stay put, we get to Second Earth, and nothing has to come of it, right? The sharks will eventually starve in there."

Joslin agreed. "Yeah. Nothing else we can do. If it's not a problem, then why make it a problem?"

Mooch could hold back the tremor in his voice. "Do you know what that pink shit really is?"

"That's the funny thing. I have no idea. Nobody will say. The only thing I know is that it's Dr. Fleming's creation. It's like a super fluid. A cross between engine coolant, motor oil, gasoline, and God knows what."

"I'm beginning to think whatever Globo Corps' reports say about Hydrolyne is a bunch of bullshit. What's with the perpetual motion crap? If I remember correctly, the reports say as long as the pink stuff is in motion, it'll act as fuel for any engine, no matter how big or small. Don't you think that's a bit...strange? If you think about the laws of physics, combustion, and common sense, don't you think there's more to this pink stuff than science? It's doing something strange to those sharks."

"We've gone beyond the realm of beakers and test tubes. This is mad science territory."

Mooch shivered. A cold finger went down his back. "Pray we can keep them contained."

"Yeah. No kidding."

Joslin and Mooch couldn't shake that unsettled feeling. That sensation creeping under their skins and riding up their spines transformed into real terror the moment the automatic doors behind them came open, and the group of armed individuals stormed into the control room.

WE'RE COMING...AGENTS OF DEATH

Listen to my words, loyal followers. We are God's elite. The holiest of men and women. We are all disciples of his will. We flinch not in the face of a challenge. Judgment and atonement awaits us all on the other side. His will. His way. We need not pray, for his word has been inside of us since we were birthed from the wombs of our mothers. God speaks to us, and us only, because He knows we are prepared to spread his gospels through brotherhood, tithing, kindness, determination, joy, sorrow, life...and bloodletting.

You work in mysterious ways, o' Lord, our Savior. How appropriate that we deliver this fate to those aboard The Redeemer. He has called for the end of Earth. For it is his will.

Those who subvert our maker's will shall pay an even greater penance than those previously burned on Earth. We're coming for you. One by one, you will perish.

Oh Holy one, we are your agents of death. Everybody's blood will be spilled, until there is not a single human heart left beating. Blood, o' Lord, we give to you, this generous tithing.

All shall perish.

We are the agents of death.

We are coming for you.

Heaven is our final destination.

GIVE THE TOUR, ERNIE PINE!

Douche bag. Cocksucker. Bullshit artist. Go jump up your own ass and see how it smells in there. I'm sure it stinks as much as your breath, Mr. Pine. Keep on talking. I got the jump on you.

Ernie Pine stood above Ram on an escalator. They were working their way up from the ground floor of *The Redeemer* ship. Ernie narrated the tour as they went up each floor with cheesy gusto. Ram couldn't help but know that behind every one of Ernie's words lurked murder.

"*The Redeemer* is forty stories of cutting edge science. The patrons on this ride only have access to half the ship. The rest is complicated machinery, and a lot of other nonsense that'll mix up even the smartest guy around."

Ram took it all in. The area was simply amazing. He imagined a cross between a super mall and an indoor resort. Each level formed a large circle with a barrier to look down to the very first floor. This was a mega mall in space.

"You go this way, we've got a food court with elaborate seating. You want steak and eggs, you want the finest Italian cuisine, maybe enjoy some seafood, or if you just want a peanut butter and jelly sandwich, our topnotch chefs will whip it up for you in a blink.

"On the next level, you'll enjoy a bunch of fun. We've got the largest indoor swimming pool with a built-in wave pool. If you didn't think about it, you'd think you were on a real beach. We've got sand, Tiki bars, and the whole nine yards.

"There's also a shopping area. Everybody on board received a voucher. You can buy clothes, apparel, and the finest jewelry.

We've got real estate salesman showing the kinds of housing on Second Earth. They're all amazing feats of architecture. Just you wait and see. We'll have something real special for you, Ram. The things you can do with glass and plastics. All thanks to Globo Corps."

Yeah, whatever, you fucking dick. Keep talking. I'll act like I care.

"On the next level, you got your upscale suites. Our rooms will have everything you'll ever need. You'll see soon enough, Ram. You're getting the gold standard suite. Only the best, for the best."

Ram couldn't wait until Ernie was finished with this brag-a-thon crap. He enjoyed a healthy paycheck playing for the NFL for six seasons as a leading quarterback, but he didn't consider himself one to relish himself in lavish things. He didn't own a mansion with a Porsche for every member of the household and a gold watch for both hands. Helen was good like that. Ram's wife was a real person, and the sight of big money didn't change that.

Thinking about Helen almost brought him to tears.

Ram forced it down. He couldn't afford to miss a single moment standing near Ernie Pine. This was life or death. Thinking about regrets could come later, if he lived long enough to look back at the past and conquer it.

Ram did his best to react impressed. "It's very...overwhelming. In a good way, Mr. Pine. Very fine accommodations here. I'm impressed."

"Call me, Ernie. We're friends. And don't forget, I still owe you an apology for the way you were treated earlier. There's no excuse."

Ram pretended to shrug it off. "I'm here, and I'm alive, so what's there to be sorry about?"

Ernie wasn't sure how to respond to that, so he smiled that car salesman's grin and continued the orated tour.

"Above the guest's quarters, we have an extensive collection of bars, wine tasting rooms, and beyond that, places to walk freely and look at outer space. It's an amazing view. You want to see outer space?"

"Who doesn't?"

For the first time, Ram spoke honestly. He did want to see where *The Redeemer* had taken them.

They kept moving up the escalator until they reached the thirty-seventh floor. The escalator directed them onto a circular track made of the softest green Astroturf. The track was surrounded by thick Plexiglas walls showcasing outer space. People talked animatedly, pointing at the views in awe and wonderment. Many were holding wine flutes, beer mugs, and smoking fine cigars. They were dressed in high end clothing. Ram imagined them attending a ball at the White House. Ram felt like a standout eyesore in his Rams football jersey and faded blue jeans and sneakers. He was a schmuck among the wealthy one percent.

Ernie directed him to the nearest wall. He pointed out the planets among the deep black backing of the solar system. Jupiter. Uranus. Mercury. Saturn. The suited ass kisser went on and on about infinity, and how far they were from Earth, and how nobody else had taken this many people, on this big of a ship, with this many fancy accommodations, to space. NASA paled in comparison to Globo Corps' advancements.

Ernie's words meant very little to Ram.

Words were a joke compared to the sights.

What Ram's eyes beheld was overwhelming. Ram couldn't stop taking in the immensity of the solar system. They had left Earth behind, because Earth was no more. Anything could happen on the way to Second Earth. This ship was the only thing between survival and the end of humanity.

Ram's head buzzed with pain. The blow to his head was still bothering him. The voltage to his body also stayed with him. The feeling of electricity in his veins remained unsettling. As unsettling as knowing the man talking to you was planning to kill you the first chance he got.

The only way to work past this strange moment was to keep talking.

"What we survived is horribly miraculous. It's amazing anybody could build a ship that could take us to another planet. The fact Globo Corps established another planet is amazing."

Ernie seemed to take off his false front and spoke candidly. The change was chilling. The man's eyes were deep black pools of cynicism. Ernie leaned in real close to Ram and kept his voice barely above a whisper. The man didn't want anybody around them to hear a word coming out of his mouth.

"Honestly, Ram, this wasn't a humanitarian affair. This ship was only meant for the world's elite to have their own planet to live on. The billionaires who were bored of spending money on things available in boutiques, or even the illegal things on the black market. Alligator skin apparel and flecks of gold on your cake don't get these people off anymore. What's the point in spending the money you earned if you can't find anything interesting to buy, am I right?

"I understand their situation. You reach the pinnacle in the capitalistic system, and you crave new things to obtain. That's where I come in, Ram. I work for Bryce Saxon. He's the president of Globo Corps. You haven't met him yet. Mr. Saxon and I act as liaisons for these ultra-rich clients to find new ways to burn their money. Call us mega brokers.

"I'm not talking about expensive housing, or buying an island. I'm talking about the purchasing of an entire planet. Then the creation of this space ship. Then real estate on the new planet. It goes on and on. Once we presented this project to the right people, everything seemed to fall into place. Strange how that worked out. Reports kept piling up about how Earth's time was about up. Mother Nature was going to hit the self-destruct button, and we were all going to burn.

"And that made more sales and commissions for me. That fear is the engine of commerce. It's all gold in my bank. Our clients wanted quick access to *The Redeemer*, so we built hovercrafts to get them there that were fire and heat resistant. They wanted to have a good time on the way to their new home, so we added the many special features aboard this fine vessel.

"This wasn't a great plan to save humanity. It was flawed out the ass. We didn't realize how close we were cutting it to being cooked crispy. This was just a way for rich people to get their gold rocks off. Bottom line. The truth. I shit you not, Ram."

A female waiter in a gold sparkling outfit was walking by the groups of people with wine flutes full of sparkling champagne. Ernie grabbed one for himself and Ram.

Ernie extended his flute in cheers. "Get some booze in you, buddy. You're going to be glad-handing and chatting up our guests in a few moments."

Use me, Ram thought. *Go ahead. I'm going to make you jump off sides, and when you do, I'll throw you down so hard, you'll break into a million pieces.*

"Come on, Ram. Let's meet the guests."

Ram followed Ernie across the soft faux grass track until they reached an open-air bar where hundreds of people were waiting for him to make an appearance.

It had been two long years since he had received this much fanfare.

Ram would have to enjoy it, while it lasted.

Football, the cool space ship, and Second Earth wouldn't matter in the face of what was coming their way very soon.

PART THREE: HIJACKED

NO CHANCE TO BE BRAVE

"You can't do this! Consider the people you're putting in danger. Yourselves included!"

Mooch couldn't process what had happened in a matter of minutes in the control room. The dozen people in the room wore a mix of fine suits, nice dresses, and cutting edge styles only serious money could afford. The group was heavily armed with a variety of weapons. Machetes. Scythes. K-bar knives. M-16s. AK-47s. K-1200 riot-style 12 gauges. Colt AR-15 Carbines. MZ-14 Bullpups. Each of the mixed members of the group had large holy crosses drawn in their foreheads in what had to be blood. The way it dried on their skin, it was a grungy orange-brownish color.

Mooch feared for himself and Joslin. What were these people going to do to them? Joslin couldn't speak, so Mooch did the talking.

"What do you people want from us?"

The group's eyes were trained on one man. He was bald, roughly one-hundred and fifty pounds, tall and lanky, and had that religious zealot look about him. The kind of look that said 'I will crucify the world in the name of my insanity'.

This man stepped up to the control panel. He clutched a machete in one hand. This man's voice was thick with evil intentions. This man, this figurehead, had spoken brainwashing words to hundreds.

"What is going on in that room?"

Mooch swallowed hard. "This is where the fuel to the ship gets processed. It's the engine of the ship. It's why we're able to travel in space at such high speeds."

"*No*," the man said angrily. "What are those poor creatures doing in those pipes? I see sharks, I see fish, and I see life submerged in pink chemicals. How dare you? Nothing surprising here. Globo Corps has no scruples. Why couldn't they let God's will be done? You subvert God's word by building *The Redeemer*. You rape nature. This was supposed to be the end of the world. I demand you release these creatures at once and let them live their lives naturally. There is a way of things, and you, along with Globo Corps, have perverted them."

"Are you nuts?" Mooch couldn't believe what this crackpot jackpot was asking him. "You can't let them out. Look, I didn't put them there. When Globo Corps pumped water out of the ocean, they accidentally—"

The handle of the machete struck the top of Mooch's head. He dropped from his chair, slammed onto the ground, and lost his ability to see and breathe until firm hands lifted him back up into his chair.

The leader demanded again, "I said let them out. I'm not asking. You will do as I say."

Mooch's faculties returned, add to that a hot streak of anger. The bastard tried to crack his skull open, and he damn well came close to succeeding.

"The only way you could logically free the sharks is to open up the fresh water connections that feed into the engine. The water circulates into the same system, between filters and special barriers. It's all connected, but to mix the two, you'd have chemicals and, and, and sharks mixing with the plumbing and drinking water lines. You'd be insane to do such a thing! You'd destroy the ship. I won't help you. Joslin won't either. I refuse— *gaaaaaaaaaaaaaak!*"

Joslin sprang out of her chair. She flicked open a butterfly knife from an ankle strap, slid the blade across Mooch's neck so hard, it created a great spurting yawn.

She kept stabbing, slicing, and hacking at Mooch's neck until the effort decapitated him.

Mooch didn't know what hit him, even after his lights went out, and his head bounced on the floor.

Joslin had to stop.

She was out of breath.

Her wrist and fingers hurt from clutching the knife so hard. She had literally punched her dead partner with the implement. Once Mooch lost his head, she kept sticking him in the chest. Blood was dripping everywhere. She was sick of pretending to be one of Globo Corps' goons.

She wasn't a corporate goon. She was God's warrior. Her congregation had hidden for days in the cargo bay waiting for *The Redeemer* to take off, and now, God's word would be upheld. The end of humanity was now. They would see to it until the last heart stopped beating.

"Red Revolution is here," Joslin rasped. "We shall deliver humanity into the arms of the lord. His will shall be done. On Earth, *as it is in space.*"

Mercy Lazar, the leader of the Red Revolution, the keeper of God's will, rubbed his hand in Mooch's still-burbling neck stump blood until his hands were dripping red. He drew a cross on Joslin's forehead.

"You've done us proud. All the hard work living among them, becoming one of them, has paid off. I want you to free those wonderful creatures from their chemical prisons. This is his will, and it shall be done."

"It wasn't easy. I only wanted to make you and everybody else proud."

Mercy held her face with both sticky red hands delicately. "You have. Very much so. Now free our poor creatures before we finish everybody else on the ship."

Joslin pushed aside the chair with Mooch's headless body. The corpse was flung onto the floor and struck the ground with a wet sound. She went to work at the control panel. She unlocked four clean water channels that fed into the engine room. Once those channels were opened, the pipes in the guts of the ship, the pink mess, flowed into the rest of the ship's water supply. When she turned off the filters, terminating any suction, the sharks were free to swim about *The Redeemer*.

"You did wonderfully," Mercy said. "The ship will not reach Second Earth. Now it is time to execute those on board who have subverted the will of our lord and savior. Everyone must die. *Our hands will be wet with so much blood.*"

SHARK SWIM

Instinct told them what to do within the confines of the vast network of piping. The pink colors surrounding them no longer forced them to swim one way or another. They were free to move, and the sharks did just that.

They should be near death, but instead, their bodies raged with new impulses. Savage hunger. Furious power. The lust for blood was elevated ten-fold. The longer they went without food, the more fevered they were in their need for meat. Things that once ate vegetation or other fish now craved ALL meat.

New abilities accompanied this hunger. Thicker skin. Muscle as hard as steel. New teeth, now jagged, sharper, and freakishly large, allowed them to devour their victims with cruel precision. Digestive systems were altered and advanced. Their insides seemingly had recreated themselves for new tasks unknown to lower forms, but soon to be showcased to those on board this vessel.

The further the collection of marine life plundered forward, their instincts told them they would have to use unusual methods to reach their prey.

The swarm swam through the networks of tubing and delivered them to different parts of *The Redeemer*. They could sense voices speak through walls, hear hearts beat, circulatory systems pump blood, and feel the heat pulse off of living, fresh meat.

The guts they would devour.

The hunger they would quench.

Insatiable and unstoppable.

The hunt was on.

GLAD-HAND RAM

Ram was shaking hands, hugging fans, and talking about his career as an award-winning quarterback. Liquor was flowing as the jovial conversations spread. Ram was standing in front of a water fountain with statues of mermaids posing on a tropical island. People kept asking him how good it felt to throw that pigskin in the face of Jake Lazar, that dirty terrorist. Ram didn't tell them his true feelings. He didn't relish in being a murderer. Ram edited out the aftermath of his actions, and how Red Revolution stalked him, and—

"Ram Rogan! So nice to meet you. Let me shake your hand."

Ram recognized the voice.

He's Samoan!

There was the man who was talking to Ernie Pine when Ram pretended to be unconscious in the medical ward. Ram could see him coming, and if Ernie was a greedy car salesman, Bryce Saxon was the seedy guy who handed out quarters at quarter peep show booths in the bad part of town. Bryce's skin was suitcase leather tan, his teeth bleached neon white, and every inch of him gleamed with a fresh coat of lotion sheen. If the bastard sat on a metal fold-out chair, he'd slide right off of it.

When Ram shook hands with Bryce, Ram knew he was shaking hands with the devil. Ernie's eyes harbored evil. Bryce's eyes seethed with hell's darkness.

"You're a hero, Ram. One of America's finest. We are lucky to have you aboard *The Redeemer*."

Bryce said this, and much more. He projected to the crowd, as if saying "Ram's a good guy, and so I am, because I'm standing right here next to him, right?"

One of the security officers dressed in all black fatigues with thick bullet proof vests, and this time without the helmet, took Bryce and Ernie aside. Ram could see the changes in both their faces. Their overconfidence deflated into fear.

The men were petrified, but of what?

The security officer escorted them away from the water fountain and the crowd of people without an explanation. New security officers joined them the further they moved away from the party.

Ram kept shaking hands, sharing football stories, and did his best to cheer up those who'd seen hell and had survived it.

When the crowd calmed down, Ram heard a distinct voice.

"Hey, All-American. You care to talk to a Pee Wee like me?"

Buffy was enjoying a bloody mary at the bar.

Ram joined her.

"If the Pee Wee team all looked like you, I think I'd quit the NFL and join up with you guys."

"Does it feel weird to have people wanting to shake your hand and meet you?"

"Actually, yes. I haven't played football in years. I've fallen off the radar. I'm washed up."

"Why did you quit football?"

"That's a hard question to answer."

"Try me."

Buffy was really interested in him. Everybody wanted to talk about the game, that special Super Bowl, but of his real personal life, not so much.

"I could tell you about it, but I don't want to go into it with so many people around. It's very personal."

Buffy realized she might've entered painful territory. "Sorry, Ram. You don't have to tell me anything you're not comfortable with. I know we just met."

"It's different with you," Ram said. "You've seen me at my most vulnerable. When I was unconscious, I mean."

"You're saying me seeing you that way was like five dates?"

"So this is a date?"

Buffy smiled.

Ram smiled back.

There was a scream.

The crowd at the bar was in an uproar. Ram and Buffy searched for the source of the concern, running towards the commotion. The water fountain at the bar had changed. What was flowing out of the water system was now a neon pink color. The concoction boiled. One older lady was clutching at her arm. What was left of it. Her fingers had melted off, and her wrist was a boiling circle of meat. She was screeching in agony. Security guards grabbed her, and urged her away.

"She needs help!" Buffy shouted. She pushed forward through the crowd. "I'm a nurse. I can help. Let me through!"

One of the guards turned to her. "Stay back, ma'am. This is under our control. You'll be notified, if you're needed."

"There's no other medical personnel on the ship. I don't know what you're going to do for the poor lady. At least let me take a closer look at her. You have to—"

"Back off, lady!"

One guard raised his baton at her.

Ram grabbed Buffy by both arms. "Come on. I know how this will end. You know the story too. They won't hesitate to knock you out."

"Did you see that poor woman's hand? It's horrible. I have to help her. Why would they turn away my assistance?"

"I don't know, Buffy, but it's not wise to go up against them when we're unarmed. I already know that Ernie Pine asshole's got a plan for me. I'm beginning to think the people who run this ship are a bunch of psychos."

"What do you mean Ernie has a plan for you?"

Ram took Buffy by the hand. "I'll tell you somewhere private."

"How about my room?"

He let Buffy lead the way.

The poor woman's screams faded with each new step they tread.

DEAD BODY

Ernie Pine knew in this moment that his one-way trip to Second Earth wasn't going to be a smooth one. This pleasure ride had quickly demurred into an emergency situation. He stood beside Bryce Saxon in Gaby Reigns' room. The dead woman hung from a shower rod by the neck. Her stomach had been slit open, and her intestines fashioned into a pseudo-noose. Crimson crosses were drawn along the tiles and mirrors in the bathroom. Gaby had called in room service, and when she didn't answer the door, the call boy entered and found her dead. Ernie and Bryce were notified by security of the situation. Ernie had to see it for himself. He still couldn't believe someone had been murdered. Especially like this.

A psycho was on board, Ernie thought. Maybe several nut jobs. The end of the world could do strange things to people. He'd seen many people unhinged on this ship, but after a stiff drink or a handful of pills, they came back to themselves.

Not whoever did this.

Ernie was speechless.

Bryce knew what to do. He was alarmingly confident. "Call in Pathfinder 3000. Him and his boys will track down this menace and kill them with extreme prejudice. That's all there is to it. I thought we'd make it to Second Earth without any hiccups. I guess I was wrong. This kind of shit creeps me out. God freaks."

Ernie was rubbing his aching head. So many problems had cropped up at once. "Yeah, let's talk more about those hiccups. We're in serious trouble, even if we stop this character who murdered Gaby. What about the pink water situation? The pilots on the ship say our engine room is compromised. We're running on back-up power. They say the ship has four hours maximum before we run out of fuel. Then we drift in space aimlessly until the air gets used up, and this craft becomes a floating tomb."

"The way you talk sometimes, Ernie. You could tone it down a bit. You're talking in front of a corpse."

"Oh, Mr. Morality over here. We're not exactly innocent. Our plan involved some serious blood spilling later on. Still might, actually."

"Shut your mouth. Yeah, okay, I'm evil. But my evil is a necessary one. Gaby's death...was more of a recreational thing. The get off on it kind of thing. I'm doing this for sound reasons. Survival. Improvement. The future. All of that. I'm not crazy. I don't jerk off to this shit!"

Ernie almost laughed at Bryce's defensiveness. "I helped you make these decisions, so whatever you are; I'm the same exact thing. You don't have to justify yourself to me. They're waiting for us to make a decision on what to do next, up in the pilot's quarters. What should I tell them? Declare an emergency?"

"The plan's the plan," Bryce said. "Nothing has changed. Except the way we get to Second Earth. There was always a Plan B. We don't declare an emergency. We contact those we planned to actually de-board this ship from the beginning, and we get them to safety. Everybody else that's expendable, they can take this on however they like. They're on their own. First thing, this killer has to be found and taken out."

"Of course, sir. I'll call Pathfinder 3000."

Ernie and Bryce stepped into the hallway to discover the two security guards standing outside the door were dead on the ground. Each had slashes bleeding across their throats. There stood two men in street clothes beside the bodies. Each of them had red crosses of blood painted on their foreheads.

"*We are here to guide you to true salvation.*"

"*Step into the arms of the lord.*"

"*Blood for blood.*"

"*A pound of flesh, for a pound of flesh.*"

"*The Red Revolution is here.*"

Bryce was blasted twenty-five times with an M-16. It happened in seconds. Bryce's feet left the ground. He was thrown back eleven feet. When he landed, the man was already a dead, pulped out mess with horror blaring out of his still open eyes.

Ernie retreated to the nearby elevator, pumped the button to close it, and thanked God when it shut. He somehow managed to outrun the two crazed killers.

He missed death by a fraction of a second.

Ernie knew death's shroud would try to cover him again very soon.

He used the phone next to the elevator buttons to call that very special person.

Pathfinder 3000.

MOMENT OF CALM

STAY IN YOUR ROOMS. PLEASE FOLLOW OUR INSTRUCTIONS FOR YOUR SAFETY. DO NOT LEAVE UNTIL OTHERWISE NOTIFIED. FOR YOUR SAFETY, PLEASE FOLLOW ALL INSTRUCTIONS. DO NOT LEAVE YOUR ROOMS.

The automated voice announced this over the intercoms spread out among each of the guest's rooms. Ram listened to it and couldn't help shaking his head in concern. Buffy was sitting on the bed with her head in her hands. She was going to collapse against the stress of the situation if he didn't do something.

Ram needed words to comfort her. People always expected him to take action and to have the answers. Even back in the days when he was a professional quarterback, if they lost a game, if a play failed, or if their team wasn't an efficient point-scoring machine, the blame was all put on him. The quarterback.

Leadership was the word. Keeping it together, being another. He didn't have the luxury of tears or emotions until the game was over.

And this fucked up game was only the beginning.

Ram decided to lay it out on the line.

"Ernie Pine and Bryce Saxon plan to kill me before we land on Second Earth. I'm not supposed to be here. I pretended to be unconscious in the infirmary, before you arrived in the medical ward, and I heard those two ass clowns talk. They were going on about how I was Samoan, and I would mate with all the women, and throw a wrench in their plan. They talked about me like I was some kind of an ape.

"Those two are crazy. They want to control the future. Who would've thought when the world ended, there'd still be an evil corporation running things?

"They said my death would look like an accident. I was to lift the morale of those on board during the ride, and once we got there, I'd punch in my final ticket."

Buffy's eyes were swollen with tears. Nothing he said was making her feel better.

"Okay, I'll try this again. I'm sticking with you, Buffy. Whatever happens. I don't want you to get caught up in the crossfire when they come gunning for me. I can hide on the ship somewhere. I'll find you later. But I'll stay with you as long as you want me here. I'll do what I can to keep you safe. I don't want you killed because of your association with me."

Buffy gave him a high pitched cackle and couldn't stop laughing. "Oh, you'll keep me safe, huh? Yes. Of course. A man. A football hero. Your machismo will shield me from fire hot enough to melt you down to liquid. You'll block that pink liquid that melted that poor woman's arm earlier from sizzling off my flesh? Your cock will block certain danger from touching me. Oh mighty cock! Bow down to your fleshy edifice!"

"That's not what I mean, Buffy. Goddamn it. This isn't a testosterone dance. I care about you. I know we only just met. I consider you a friend. I want you to survive. I don't want you to get hurt because of me."

Buffy's mania didn't relent.

"You want what's best for me, because you care for me? Is that it? You want to save me, so I owe you, and you can control me later on? No thanks, Ram. Forget it. You can keep everything you have to offer me."

"No, Buffy. I'm only saying I want you to be safe. You owe me nothing. I am your friend. That's it. I swear to you. I don't know where you're coming up with this other stuff. You're wrong about me."

Buffy's eyes changed. They were moving fast back and forth. She was working through something toxic and hurtful. She pulled out a cigarette, struck a match, and pulled on it hard.

"You sound like my late husband. He said what he did was all in the interest of protecting me. He knew what was best for me. That implies I don't know what's best for myself. I'm not a fragile thing. I'm a woman. I'm not a child.

"My dead husband used to be a nice man. I met him in college. He later became a Beverly Hills surgeon. One of those surgeons of the stars. Lips, breasts, ass, tummy tucks, you name it, he could do it, and he got paid handsomely for it.

"We had a strong marriage for the first couple of years. That was until he starts spouting that horrible end of the world nonsense. Everybody's been on edge with the talk of it hitting the news, but some people go over that edge. Everybody was saying pollution, global warming, the thinning of the ozone, and how all of it had finally caught up with us.

"There's no real explanation for the Earth burning up. If there was somebody who could explain it, they're probably dead now. But the change in my husband was alarming. He wasn't himself. He had rich friends who were pumping ideas into his mind. I knew this when I found the Globo Corps pamphlets in his study. I wasn't supposed to go in that room. I didn't care. I was losing the man I loved, and I had to do something about it.

"The pamphlets were about buying real estate on Second Earth. Globo Corps offered to save you from the nightmares of the apocalypse if you invested so many millions of dollars to their cause. There were pictures of hovercrafts, and how they'd mail you a silver blanket to protect you from the fire and acid rain. Then those bulky plastic watches. They are tracking devices.

"There were facts about approximately when the Earth would destroy itself. It's scary how on the money they were about that fact. Our government couldn't pin it down, but Globo Corps could, with their mega money and insane resources.

"Globo Corps sounds like a scary giant," Ram said. "I know very little about them, and being here on this ship, they already give me the creeps."

"Creepy is a good word. This was the first I knew of my husband's interest in Globo Corp, and Second Earth. The information was so...fantastic. I was terrified reading it. These people sounded like fanatics, and that's what they are.

"I dug around in my husband's office and located receipts and paperwork. He had lots of investments in the stock market. He donated well over ten million dollars to Globo Corps. Maybe more. I never knew exactly how much money he threw at them. But that's not the worst of it.

"He had pictures, drawings, weight, diet details, and vitals on me. He must've put my doctor up to getting that information. I was a slab of meat. Every inch, crevice, and cavity was explained in fine detail in this thick manila folder. Imagine a physical in drawings, pictures, charts, and all the gory details."

"Why would he have all of that info on you?"

"It turns out my husband had sent these, and more, to Globo Corps for processing. They want to start over on Second Earth. Globo Corps wants women. Not just any women, but hearty women who bleed the richest milk from their tits. Women who can give birth to dozens of children. Women who can pass on the finest genes, hair color, eye color, you name it. Globo Corps enjoyed my portfolio so much, they guaranteed us two tickets on *The Redeemer*.

"My husband caught me rooting around through his things one day. He flew into a rage. It was the first time he ever hit me. This wasn't just a slap. He beat me until I was bleeding. He said I had to go on a special diet. He wanted me to keep my weight down, take all of these crazy vitamins, and run so many miles a day. He said if I told anybody about Globo Corps, or tried to leave him, he'd kill me, and my family. I was scared of him. He would follow up on everything he said. I knew he wasn't lying.

"After a month or two of this harassment, I was determined to leave him anyway. Then the ground starts spewing fire. Before we can be picked up by those hovercrafts, my husband falls into a hole into the ground, and he lands in a pool of hot magma shit. I'm still saved, and they wanted to use my skills as a nurse on the ship. I agreed. But I know once we're on that planet, they expect me to open my legs and pump out baby after baby. I won't do it. I'll hide from them. I'll kill myself."

"No," Ram snarled. "You won't kill yourself. I'll help you hide from them. I don't want to be a part of their plan either, and they don't want me anyway. My Samoan blood would taint their gene pool. They can go fuck themselves. I wasn't offering anything to those bastards. I wouldn't give them my semen if they put a gun to my head."

Buffy remained cold, and that distant look in her eye proved she was sinking deeper and deeper into herself.

"There's no saving anybody, Ram. You mean well. Everybody means well. But you're nothing against Globo Corps. They hold the cards. They are the cards. They're...everything. Try and survive, Ram. That's all there is."

"Just let me try to help you, okay? Enough of this dark bullshit. We're not surrounded by fire anymore."

"Yeah, we're not. We're just up in space, surrounded by nothing. This ship is a trap. This is really it. The end. Nothing will be the same. Everybody I once knew is dead. The future is as uncertain as it gets."

Ram held her close. "It's overwhelming. Everything is terrible. You can't erase this tragedy. All you can do is...keep on. Be grateful for every moment of life you get. Many didn't get that luxury back on Earth. We're fortunate."

Something new gleamed in Buffy's eyes.

"You're right. We're very lucky."

"You have to take advantage of every second you get," Ram continued. "Live life to the fullest. It might sound like a bunch of self-help crap, but it's true. I had a big tragedy in my life occur too, and that's what I learned. Take advantage of our second of life you have, no matter the circumstances."

Buffy held Ram's face with two gentle hands.

His words were finally connecting with her.

She whispered to him, "*I want you to make love to me.*"

PART FOUR: HUNGRY SHARKS

PILOT'S QUARTERS

The ten person crew piloting *The Redeemer* knew they had their backs against the wall. The Engine Control Room was compromised. The bloody video feed proved that much. Mooch was murdered by a band of religious crazed marauders, and Joslin, that bitch traitor, was a part of the attack. However the religious group snuck onto the ship, they wanted everybody on board dead. And that was only the beginning of their problems.

Gregory Hawker, the lead pilot, faced his crew and knew doom was looming over them. The ship's oil, the pink stuff, was flowing into the fresh water pipes and plumbing. The chemical was cycling throughout the ship. And whatever sea life had been sucked up by Globo Corps' band of assholes was loose among the guest quarters.

The question now was damage control. With the fuel spreading about the ship the way it was, there was no way of replacing it. They were currently running on back-up power. Battery cells, actually. Those would last fours hours, tops. The ship wasn't going to make it to Second Earth. Without fuel, the ship would drift aimlessly until they ran out of air.

There was still a chance somebody could make it to Second Earth. The emergency ships could take a limited number of people to safety. Hawker believed he could lead an organized effort to rescue as many people as possible and do just that.

Whatever the outcome, Hawker couldn't stand by and watch his fellow pilots cry like babies wearing shit-stuffed diapers.

"Okay, wipe your asses. We're not dead yet. We've got a job to do. The people on this ship are counting on us to make good decisions. Humanity doesn't stop here. Not if I got something to say about it.

"That pink shit is highly toxic. It'll melt you down. But if it's diluted down with water, it won't be as harmful, as long as it's not ingested. I can turn up the water pressure. It'll make the water escaping from the burst pipes flow in higher quantities. We'll have some rivers and streams on the ship. It's all to buy us time. Whoever opened the flood gates in the engine room wanted this to happen. So we'll work with it.

"I'm putting this ship on auto pilot. I'm also programming the emergency ships to fly out to Second Earth once they're engaged. The people are going to be panicked. Tell them to pile in those emergency ships, shut the hatch, and they will automatically start a course to Second Earth. Easy as cooking a frozen dinner in a microwave.

"Everybody else, I want you to round up the passengers and direct them towards the Floor Zero port."

"Not everybody's going to fit on those emergency ships," one of Hawker's subordinates said. "What do we do then? They'll already be freaking out. It'll be chaos."

"Not everybody's going to make it from Point A to Point B. You've got those religious psychos parading about the ship, that pink melty shit dripping everywhere, and man-eating sea creatures. Don't worry about that problem. Just get people moving to Floor Zero. Whoever makes it in one piece will have the honor and distinction of living on Second Earth.

"I will make the announcement over the intercom that we've got an emergency situation on our hands. Now everybody get moving. Get your heads out of your *asses*, and go save some!"

Hawker's crew hurried to their appointed tasks.

After setting *The Redeemer* on auto pilot, and turning up the water pressure in the plumbing, the control panel burst into flying sparks and chunks of broken screens and computer boards. Before Hawker could react, a tiger shark's mouth surged through the panel. The shark chomped on his arms up to the elbows.

Hawker fell back with two spurting nubs for arms. Before he could feel the pain, the same shark was lifted from the control panel by a burst of faded pink water. The tiger shark's dark eyes focused on Hawker. Those jagged teeth, so numerous, so long, so sharp, so hungry, so mutated, closed in for the kill.

The deadly mouth swallowed him whole. Hawker's body was twisted upside down, right side up, as working muscles forced him down the monster's throat.

When he landed in the shark's belly, Hawker splashed into a purple-black pool of water. Half digested bodies surrounded him. Some people were intact and alive. Hands grabbed for him. Bodies drew Hawker close to them. They were embracing him for comfort, for the process of being digested alive in the shark's belly was excruciating, and ever so slow.

Hawker prayed for death.

His prayers were eventually answered.

WHAT'S COOKIN'?

Juan Hernandez was very familiar with fine cooking. He had been head chef at a variety of five star restaurants. Only the best and premiere cuisine. Juan was confident in his culinary abilities. His team, whoever Globo Corps had dug up in a hurry, were a bunch of hot shot wannabes. Some were solid workers, but when over half of your staff were worthy of scooping shit onto a plate at some cheap buffet, the final product suffered.

Juan's headache hadn't stopped since the world burned up. He lost everything, including his family, his house in Beverly Hills, and his restaurant. Now, he was worried about losing his sanity. He stood in the fridge alone to gain a moment of clarity. When his restaurant was busy, or when he was short-staffed and overwhelmed, it wasn't uncommon for the cooks to take a moment in the fridge or the freezer to scream, shout, and vent their frustrations. Juan had stood in the fridge long enough that he was starting to shiver.

The headache was still there, but the anger in him had ebbed. He could keep doing this. This job, this opportunity, even without his family, meant he could lead future generations into the new world. He could help teach people how to live life right. Second Earth was the biggest opportunity known to any man, woman, or child, and Juan was going to do something special with it, whether it be on a skillet, plate, or menu.

Juan charged out of the freezer with new energy.

"Okay people, we've got dinner service coming up soon. Our passengers are hungry. They've seen horrible things. We're here to take their minds off of their problems. We've got our hands full, but I'm here to help. We can do this!"

Juan realized he was talking to a lifeless kitchen.

His mouth hung open in horror.

The dish washer had been sent through the giant dish machine and was laying on the other side burned to death.

Not burned to death.

Melted.

The body was covered in pink popping fluids. Chemical burns. Peeled back flesh. Sizzling muscle tissue.

Juan's eyes scanned the room, and each new horror, with building dismay.

Ralph Cotton, the fattest, and the best cook on his staff, stood in front of a collection of tall boiling pots without a head. Ralph's head was bouncing around in a tall boiling pot of water.

Another cook, Mary Ellen, had her face shoved into an industrial sized meat grinder, and had half her head grinded down to pink bloody straw.

Chuck Buffett, the steak master, had his face pressed against the grill. His face was cooked black. A meat tenderizer had been slammed so hard into the back of Chuck's head the weapon stayed there, sunk into two inches of gray matter.

The youngest cook, Angie McConnell, had her face forced into a three-story cake and had suffocated to death. She had noticeably urinated in her pants during her sweet snuffing. Another cook had been working in front of a deep sink. Two pairs of legs up to the torso stood in place. The rest of him had seemingly dissolved into the overflowing sink. Water didn't fill the sink. A sizzling pink substance was boiling hard, promoting its ability to dissolve the human body.

Other cooks had been thrown into the trash, their stomachs carved out into grizzly hollows. Intestines hung from the ceiling's exposed pipes. Blood crosses were smeared on the walls in psychotic finger font.

Juan felt like the room was spinning.

The sights were so grotesque.

The pipes were making the strangest churning noises. Pressures were rising and falling within the steel tubes. Juan thought they could burst at any second.

Who had killed his staff?

Who drew those gnarly crosses?

This had happened in a matter of minutes. Who could perpetrate such atrocity so fast?

Juan grabbed a steak knife from a nearby rack. Anything, anybody, could rush out at him and take his life.

He didn't say a word.

Juan kept watch. His eyes were as wide as they could get. Dreams of Second Earth dissolved just like his assistant cook in that sink.

The pipes overhead kept grumbling and whining.

Steel was bending and expanding.

Underfoot, sections of the floor cracked. Tiles shattered. Trenches in the floor expanded, causing the floor to break away into four big sections.

Juan dodged the pots that crashed to the ground.

"Jesus! God!"

Cookery smashed to the floor. Juan did his best to stay stable and upright. He teetered, bent forward, almost did the splits, and called out for help.

The pipes above him exploded, showering the kitchen in foamy pink boiling hot liquid. Before Juan had a single drop touch him, the floor lifted him up two feet.

"*Whooooooooafaaaaaaaaaaahk*!"

Juan had two seconds to view what was hoisting him up into the air. Once his eyes processed the sight, it was like falling down a deep hole. Lowering down into the pitch black recess, he viewed columns of enormous teeth the size of human beings.

The jaws of the great white shark bit down on Juan. He was chewed up in a cacophony of shattering bones, shredding flesh, and popping guts.

The shark swallowed him raw.

Dinner service was cancelled.

LUXURY SUITE

"I gave up a lot to be here," Lionel Little of Little Industries, a mega billionaire importer of fine cars, bickered. "This suite is sub-standard. Our hot tub doesn't work. The mini fridge doesn't have a decent bottle of bourbon. I might as well be drinking river swill. I paid top dollar to be here. Should've considered this a ticket on public transportation. Such offense! "I'm responsible for Globo Corps' progress. My wallet was always open to those people. When they asked for more funds, I didn't say why, or how come; I only said how much? I'm being butt-fucked here, and I don't like it. I'm Lionel Little. I make Donald Trump look like a work-a-day paperboy! I won't stand for this insult!"

The sixty-year old billionaire was trying to burn a line into the carpet with his constant pacing. He didn't notice the eighteen year old *Sports Illustrated* model, Tonya Black, the blonde bombshell, splayed out on the bed nude to the toes.

The bubbly would-be Michael Bay movie star invited Lionel in that bimbo, sex me up lilt, "Come to bed, Lionel. You can drink me instead. Anything you want, big man. I'm all yours. All you can handle, baby."

Lionel was unaffected by Tonya's words.

"And you know what else? Those announcements keep telling us to stay in our rooms. I didn't pay for mistakes. I paid for a good time. I don't need this aggravation. Every time I call the help desk, the phone rings and rings. Nobody answers. And forget room service. God forbid I wish to order something on this super ship piece of shit. Globo Corps. More like Globo Whore."

Tonya was pressing her double-d implants together. "It's not such a bad thing being trapped in our room together, is it?"

She tweaked her nipples, and threw her head back in delight. She chewed on the ends of her bleached blonde hair and gave him that sexy stare. Tonya knew how it transformed *Mr. Little* into *Mr. Big*. The model utilized everything in her cannon to calm her high strung mega rich husband. She posed, and was about to play with herself, when Mr. Little stormed towards the wall in a fit of rage.

"I bet the flat screen TV doesn't work. Let me turn it on, and we'll see."

Tonya screamed in horror. The TV seemed to leap off the wall. The plaster behind it exploded. A giant hammerhead shark shot forth. The shark's mouth bit Lionel on his torso. Then a wicked *crunch* sound. Lionel landed in two pieces on the floor. Another mouth, a lemon shark, burst through the carpet and swallowed his legs, taking the extra time to crack through those thick knee caps. Lionel's top half evaporated into the pink frothing waters that spilled into the room from the growing hole in the ceiling.

Tonya stayed glued to the bed. The levels of boiling pink waters were so high, the bed was floating. She did her best to stay on the melting island. The bed itself was beginning to disintegrate and burn. Above her horrified screams, the pipes in the ceiling groaned. They were bending, expanding, and finally bursting. A wall of twenty ravenous barracudas and mixed fish latched onto Tonya's body. The only thing left of her supple body after the devouring were her implants.

SECURITY FORCE

Tom "Shrapnel" Wilson dropped everything when the lights in the security quarters glowed from white to a deep red.

WARNING. THREATS DETECTED ON EVERY LEVEL. SECURITY REQUESTED IMMEDIATELY.

The automated warning on the room's intercom had everybody going. Shrapnel didn't hesitate. He stubbed out his cigarette, threw on his riot gear, and tried not to crash to the floor. Shrapnel had shared two bottles of Jack Daniels among his twelve person crew.

"Move it, Taz. Put down that microwave burrito and get your lazy ass into gear. Our passengers need our help. Load up, and gear up."

Blazer and Reeds had been bumping uglies in the other room. One was rosy-faced, Shrapnel noticed, and the other, walked funny from the terrible affliction of blue balls.

Damn it, Shrapnel thought. These people weren't ready to fight. They thought they had an easy ride to Second Earth. No hiccups. That hypothesis was proving not to pan out at all. As Dodger, Clutch, Tiger, and Greaser changed their clothes, he could hear walls breaking, screams piercing the air, and odd sounds of things swimming and cutting through the water at high speeds.

Shrapnel would have to psych up his team to get them in the game. He noticed their best weapon, the Pathfinder 3000, hadn't been fully charged. Shrapnel took that moment to put the machine on charge and let it be. Pathfinder 3000 wouldn't be available for at least a couple of hours. It was up to him and his team to do the ass kicking today.

Shrapnel's crew fired out of the room in under ninety seconds flat. Heavily armed, mean-faced, muscles flexed, assholes clenched, they stormed the hallway. They headed towards the elevator ready to sweep each floor, starting from bottom to top.

Jogging towards the east end of the hall to pile into the elevator, Shrapnel knew his crew needed a jolt of courage. He would be the electricity in their veins, and the calcium to thicken the bones in their spines.

"Who has big balls?"

The team chimed in, "We do, sir!"

Then their song began. Each sang with the verve of a soldier of fortune with gold in his war-torn hands and a nice piece of ass on the way.

"Oh, I got balls. You know my balls are always full. Balls for you. Balls for me. Balls of fury. Balls of lightning. Balls of brass. Balls to knock up every lass up in first class. Oh, I'll empty 'em so good. Oh, I got balls. Big ol' balls."

Before the team reached the elevator, the elevator opened by itself. The song abruptly stopped. Everybody raised their guns on the offensive.

"Stand your ground," Shrapnel said. "Shoot to kill."

Everybody from his team was lifted off of their feet. Shrapnel dove, ducked, rolled, and spun in the opposite direction of the elevator in time to avoid the strange clutching things.

Tentacles, he kept thinking. Fucking tentacles.

A squid the color of a corpse dredged from the sea slithered its way out of the elevator. Its long tentacles rippled with muscles and vascular power. Each tentacle had wrapped around his team's throats. Like ripping a tab off of a beer bottle, the tentacles squeezed his team's heads off in unison. The tentacles threw up the heads into its tiny mouth and swallowed them whole.

Shrapnel thought fast, and struggled to fight off his disbelief. The squid was gigantic, and such a nebulous, evil looking creature. He threw four grenades towards the beast, lunged forward, made the turn in the hallway, and ducked for cover.

Three BOOMS later, he heard the sick squish and splatter of guts strike the walls.

"Clear," he muttered under his breath. "Fucking clear."

Before he checked to ensure nobody else had dodged the creature like he had, the wall behind him burst into pieces. He was thrown forward, and then darkness encompassed him. The air grew extra humid. Three forced flips later, he was covered in gelatin muck that burned his skin.

No!

Shrapnel peered forward through the darkness. He was looking out the mouth of a giant shark. Then that view closed, and he was further sucked down into the shark's body. He clutched at strings, muscular cables, coils of slippery wet things, and tried to fight his way forward. He was bunched up between soft walls, as his skin sizzled and burned away.

Shrapnel screamed in agony. He was bent, twisted, squashed, and downgraded into digested puddles of red. Then he was digested.

Shrapnel and his team were no more.

Security was a thing that no longer existed on the *Redeemer*.

BLOOD POOL

Tanner Simmons sat on top of his lifeguard tower watching the hundred some-odd persons swimming in the fake ocean, sunbathing on the sand under tanning lights, or mingling at the bar decorated as a giant lily pad. Tanner wasn't really a lifeguard. He couldn't give CPR. He was simply a face to a product.

Tanner Simmons was an Olympic runner who scored the gold for America. Before he could compete in the next Olympics, the earth decided to cancel everything. This was his pass to Second Earth. Meeting and greeting and hanging out at the fake beach.

What he really wanted to do was gouge out his eyes when the rich fat ass schmucks slathered themselves in suntan oil and laid out on the chairs next to their wives who could've doubled as their daughters.

Nothing but a bunch of lard asses with double bubble butts. And ladies, if you're that doughy, don't wear the tightest swim trunk bottoms. Nasty ass butt floss. And I can't stand looking at those god-awful labial split wedgies. Can't you pay someone to cut the flab off of your entitled butts? You people are rich enough.

This was the only way you were getting on The Redeemer.

You have to pay the price.

Your eyes are going to burn for a little while. At least it wasn't your ass that burned off. Be grateful, you idiot, and don't say anything stupid. Be nice.

Tanner did get the eyeballs from the ladies. That was one plus. A few had taken advantage of their drunk sugar daddy husbands who had passed out and talked to Tanner. He was chatting to one hot babe named Barbie Cunningham.

Barbie went on about how she'd love for Tanner to bust open her damn, when he saw the giant mouth rise up from the ocean and swallow three people on inflatable alligators one after the other. Two of the victims were bent awkwardly so their feet were in their faces. Tanner could hear the sound of spines breaking.

Eight fins zipped across the water, closing in on screaming swimmers. A tail lashed across a younger female swimmer. The impact caused her body to explode. Tanner saw one giant shark with the top halves of a dozen people sticking out of all sides of its closed mouth. The victims were reaching out for help as they coughed up blood.

Barbie climbed up on the lifeguard tower with him. She was shivering and crying, and she wouldn't stop telling him to "Do something, Tanner! You have to do something!"

Tanner couldn't take her squirrel shrieks a moment longer and shouted, "Bitch, what am I supposed to do about a bunch of sharks! Blow my whistle at them?"

A blue shark was slamming into the deck chairs on the beach, riding a giant wave to do so. Wood and human limbs flew across the air. A lemon shark had a three hundred pound man in his mouth and was bashing him against the sand until the man went unconscious.

"This is what we do, Barbie. We—"

Barbie was a torso in his lap. Her guts trailed down the lifeguard post and ended in a bull shark's mouth. The bull shark was sucking down the long intestines like a piece of spaghetti. Tanner clung to his seat when Barbie's lifeless torso flopped onto the ground. On the way down, her still-warm guts wrapped around his ankle.

Sucking, slurping, swallowing, and then chomping down on Barbie's top half, she was reduced to pink puree in seconds. Tanner couldn't keep his grip on the post. The shark saw he was caught by the guts, and the shark reeled him in.

Lapping up the guts even harder, the bull shark couldn't wait for Tanner to fall into his mouth. The shark lunged forward with gaping wide mouth. Tanner unleashed a terrorized yawp. It made no difference. When the shark's mouth enveloped him, darkness and teeth overtook him.

CHEWING AND SWALLOWING

Dalton Bray was showcasing his talent as a real estate agent on Second Earth. He stood in front of fifteen television screens displaying the finest housing units on the new planet, including lavish mansions, swimming pools, golden gated perimeters, a glass city, and the lush greenery Second Earth had to offer. He had already signed up ninety-eight guests for multi-million dollar properties, and he was barely half-way into his shift.

The Bray way is the only way, Dalton thought. *After this, I'm going to hit that bar with the wonderful view of space, and chase some tail. Fear always makes them wet. The Bray makes the ladies stay. The Bray way is the only way.*

He approached an older woman named Agnes Worthington. She would be a challenging client, but Dalton didn't back down. He was the best at his job. He would sell this bitch a property, easy.

When Agnes asked if Second Earth was safe, Dalton didn't hesitate. "Of course. We've had people living on the planet for many years to prove its sustainability. Nothing, I assure you, can harm you—"

Surging up from the ground, bending and warping steel, a giant bull shark passed between Dalton and Agnes. The shark moved so fast, it crashed through the ceiling and kept going to the floor below. He was about to grab his potential client and run for safety when he realized the shark's fin sliced Agnes down the middle. She had split in two. Before those two halves could land, a series of lemon sharks grabbed the halves and fought over the pieces, spreading out her guts, and playing tug of war with what wouldn't break.

Water was bursting from the walls and the many forming holes and cracks surrounding his viewing gallery of investment properties. Dalton could see sharks thrown by high-pressured jets of water swim down the escalators and gobble up those who fled on the way down.

Sharks. Giant Sharks. I can't believe it!

Dalton was about to run to the phone on the wall nearby when two hammerhead sharks collided into him from both sides. Dalton's body burst like a piñata exploded by C-4.

Wasn't it enough I had to put up with you rich fucks rubbing your successes in my face? Now I have to deal with killer sharks!

Barry Prichard was the bartender on the space viewing level of the ship. He was currently the best bartender humanity had to offer. He could whip you up a Todd Collins, a screaming orgasm, a 7 and 7, a fuzzy navel, or he could wing it and make up a new drink on the fly. Today, he would be making some drinks of the flaming variety!

Water was flooding from many directions. It lapped up against the clear panes showcasing the galaxies. Barry was ankle deep in the mess already.

He could see shark bodies punch through walls, drop from above, and somehow propel themselves across the air without the aid of water. They could throw themselves from one end of the room to the other. They weren't flying. They were pitching themselves towards their prey.

Barry reeled in shock seeing an enormous great white shark with twenty people stuffed in its mouth. The black marble gleam in the shark's eye seemed to shine with an evil zeal right before it bit down and crunched up the massacre salad.

A couple were clutching onto each other, pinned against a wall by a circle of closing in lemon sharks. Barry stuffed napkins into an open bottle of brandy, lit it with his lighter, and tossed it in their direction. The flames hit one shark on the back. The flames spread, cooking its skin. The other lemon sharks backed off from the couple.

That's when a group of five persons with crosses drawn in blood on their foreheads cut the couple up with a meat cleaver, machete, and a fire axe.

Who the fuck are those people?

Barry threw a flaming bourbon at the crazies. He got one bitch right on the head and watched her body dance with fire. She stood their taking the flames and chanting religious gibberish. *"Oh God. Oh holy, holy one! I am yours. Judge me. Take me. I am yours to have!"*

Barry hurled twenty plus bottles into the crowd of enemies, sharks and religious murderers alike. He was scattering both threats away from his position. Barry was feeling good about his stand until the cold edge of the blade was dragged across his throat.

Mercy Lazar breathed sweet nothings in the name of God into his ear until he stopped gasping and finally died.

* * *

Crissy Taylor had been on a strict diet for two years. She had lost one hundred pounds and was considered back to her ideal body weight. But when everything went to shit recently, she decided today was going to be a treat. She would stuff herself silly.

Crissy was standing at the buffet of seafood, high end steaks, and desserts tasty enough to make her cream her pants (as her late sister, Brandy, would've phrased anything that tasted good to her) when everything went into chaos. Buffet tables erupted into pieces, flinging food, glass, and hunks of wood in every direction.

The fine dining area was being attacked by water that was rushing, spilling, and blasting into the room. The tidal wave tried to mix everybody together like a washing machine's spin cycle.

Heads crashed together, killing many instantly. Others were smashed against tables and knocked unconscious. Many bled from the shards of glass mixed in with the water. Blood stained the flowing waters.

Years of strict dieting, and right before she could sink her teeth into a juicy steak, a creamy cake, or dip a piece of crab into hot butter, this bullshit had to happen! Crissy didn't care if she died. She only cared if she died with an empty stomach. She detested that feeling of empty. Fuck society. Fuck being pretty. Fuck moderation. Fuck this situation! Fuck everybody and everything!

Crissy was in such a rage, when the first shark reared its head up from the water, she didn't cower in fear. She charged forth in anger. Crissy's mouth was agape. Her jaw opened. Her mouth was as wide as it could go. Crissy leaped on top of a blue shark, clutched its fin, and bit down on its skin. She tore a piece off of its back. When the blue shark shook her off, and turned around to return the favor, Crissy would quickly regret her decision.

She wouldn't just die on an empty stomach.

She would die in a stomach.

Cleaning lady Glenda Alvarez was sprawled on top of her cleaning cart. She hopped on top when the giant wave shot her down the hallway of guest rooms. She watched the horrors that kept unfolding around her. P. F. Gould, the asshole who went out of his way to offer her a crisp fifty dollar bill for a blowjob, was being dragged by the intestines by a bull shark. Gould's body kept bashing into the walls as his dead corpse was being carried to God knew where.

Room doors kept crashing open by the powerful force of building water. Glenda screamed at the sight of a floating dead shark whose belly was being cut open from the inside and four people clawed their way out of guts and messy entrails only to be swept up in a new wave of water and carried down to another part of the ship.

The wave carrying her slowed. She was able to climb down off of the cart. Glenda ran straight for the emergency stairs. When she opened the door, she fell right into the gaping shark's maw waiting on the other side to swallow her up.

Getting off wasn't strong enough of a word. Paige Parker, known to her friends as Pretty Paige, relished in riches. She grew up a billionaire, and stayed one into adulthood. Daddy's money.

Old money.

Paige's money.

Spending it wasn't what she enjoyed.

Paige loved to steal. Five finger discounts all the way, baby.

People were running and screaming for their lives, and Paige was sneaking about the halls of the mini strip mall pilfering jewelry by the handfuls. She snagged a dress off the racks from a boutique and turned the fine attire into a sack for her lifted goods. Paige was enjoying the thrill until she saw along the display counter showcasing the many articles of gold. Among the articles was the biggest crab she'd ever seen. The ones she ate were a fraction of the size. This was as big as a Rottweiler, and those claws, they were simply HUGE.

Paige gasped in horror when she noticed the human arms, legs, and heads that had been broken off by the crab pincers. Blood and pink meat were crusted on those bizarre weapons. Paige was about to lug her take and book it out of there when four people held her down.

"Get your hands off of me! What do you think you're doing? Do you know who I am? Do you know who my dad is?"

Just in time, a small stream of water carried her father's corpse to their position. He had two carps bored into his eyes as they chewed into his brains.

"Oh God! Lemme go! Please. I'll give you anything you want!"

"Sinner!" The four accused Paige. "It's your turn to be judged!"

The tang of their bodies hit Paige, and nearly made her puke. They stank like they hadn't taken a shower in weeks and bathed in each other's bodily juices. The smell was so ripe. Paige noticed the crosses drawn in blood on their foreheads. She knew right then she'd fallen into dangerous hands.

The crab leapt off the counter and crawled towards Paige's body. They pinned her down, and Paige could only writhe and squirm as the little beast crept closer. Paige's screams joined those on board, and she too fell victim to the crab's hungry claws.

Nobody was safe.

The Redeemer truly was a death ship.

PART FIVE: FIGHT FOR YOUR LIFE

THE FUN'S OVER

Ram and Buffy made fast, needy, desperate love. This sex was in the name of getting off, and enjoying the temporary escape only flesh could provide. Quick nibbles and bites. Fast orgasms and deep satisfaction. That escape was short-lived, but so necessary. They were both winded and spent on top of the covers. They spooned each other and enjoyed the comedown.

Sex opened up people, Ram knew, and Buffy had a question to ask him. He would answer it, because he considered this woman to be the only true friend he had left in the world.

"Earlier, you said something bad happened to you. I felt better after telling you about my husband. Maybe you'll feel the same way."

"I can tell you, but it's not a pleasant story. My wife's name was Shirley. I had two kids named Brandy and Sadie. They were the best thing ever. Everything was wonderful in my life. I was being paid awesome money to throw a football. Picture it being the year the Rams went to the Super Bowl. Everything went south after I tossed that pigskin into that terrorist, Jake Lazar's, face and killed him.

"I was on every TV program being asked about my "heroic" act. I got crazy endorsement deals. The funniest one was for those strips you put on your nose so you don't snore at night. I was even in the works to sign a movie deal. I was going to become an action star. It's all ridiculous.

"So I went to parties at Hollywood A-listers' mansions. I drank, smoked, snorted, and had sex with people I didn't know. It was like a whirlwind that I got swept up into it. The drugs, the hype, it was too much for one man to handle. Everything seemed to suck me right in. It's a poor excuse for my actions. I know that, and I paid a heavy price.

"After the parties in my honor start dying down, and the news lost interest in me, and the movie deal fell through, I end up back home. When I return, I find my wife and kids dead."

Buffy gasped.

Ram's voice trembled. He wanted to break down and cry, but he had to finish the story while the words were still coming.

"My wife was hanging from the second story guardrail by her insides. She was strangled by her own..."

Ram couldn't say it. Buffy hugged him close. "You don't have to tell me."

It burst out of him. He couldn't stop.

"My kids, they were only four and five. Those Red Salvation bastards had drowned them in the bathtub. Red crosses, drawn from my wife's blood, were all over the walls in the house. It was all sickening.

"Jake Lazar's brother, Mercy Lazar, was taking revenge against me. Mercy, and a bunch of others from his cult, came after me. I narrowly escaped death by jumping out of a window. I called the police, but those awful people were already gone.

"After that, I went into hiding. I kept a low profile. I quit playing football. They offered me mega bucks, but I didn't want a penny. It was all blood money.

"I should've been home being faithful to my wife and keeping my nose clean. I would've kept them safe, or better yet, I might've died alongside them. That's how it should've gone down.

"I've lived with a lot of guilt. My mistakes cost me. That's the thing about mistakes. They burn you. They also change you. You're either the kind of person who backs down from your regrets, or you accept them. A lot of counseling has helped me along. But one thing I know for certain. If I see one of those fuckers from Red Salvation ever again, I'll kill them. Especially that rotten asshole Mercy Lazar. He's the one who leads them. He orchestrated my family's death."

Buffy couldn't say anything. The story left her lost for words. Together, they heard parts of the ship bend, creak, and shatter.

The sound of flowing and spraying water was equally disconcerting.

Screams of terror echoed throughout many of the hallways.

A message was played on the ship's intercom. They couldn't hear it over the sound of the ship breaking, except for the words EMERGENCY and SAFETY VEHICLES.

"What's going on out there?" Buffy asked. "It sounds like a war."

They got dressed. Ram was about to open the door when he heard the evil voice speak through the door.

"*Bathe in the blood of the lord. Swim to heaven in a stream of red. Die for our sins. Be reborn in heaven. The afterlife awaits you!*"

Ram's stomach turned.

He knew that voice.

Sweat burned his skin. He was breathing harder without realizing it. That voice, that horrible, murdering son-of-a-bitch!

Ram threw open the door.

Buffy rushed in behind him. "What are you doing, Ram? You're scaring me."

"Stay back, Buffy."

He wasn't ready for what he was about to see at the door. There was that tall, lanky, bald, emaciated looking monster named Mercy Lazar. Religious terrorist. Murderer.

He was dragging a machete across an old woman's neck in the hallway. Mercy's eyes lit up as she gargled on her own blood.

"God is waiting for you. Greet him with open arms. It is your destiny."

Mercy was knocked out of his moment of enlightenment when he saw Ram stand directly across from him in the hallway. The mass murderer dropped the dead woman onto the floor. She splashed down as dead weight. The floor itself was covered in three inches of flowing water and carried the corpse away.

"You."

Mercy couldn't say anything else.

"I'm glad you painted a cross on your forehead," Ram said. "You want to know why, you Bible banger?"

Mercy turned his head to the side, curiously. "Why would that be?"

"It gives me a target to punch!"

Ram turned his fist into a lethal spring-ejected battering ram. He connected with enough power and energy to knock Mercy through the door behind him. The flying man's impact caused the wood to burst from its hinges.

He was about to storm into the room and continue the beat down when from down the hall, each room's door broke open. Floods of high-pressure water sprayed into the hallway. Up from the floor, down from the ceiling, wood was bending and giving as the area was being flooded. People hiding in their rooms were forced into the hallway.

Ram's eyes went big for a new reason.

A great white shark was swimming on top of a frothing stream of fast moving water. It was coming from the very end of the hallway and right towards him. Whatever it used to be, it had transformed into a mega killing machine. The beast owned thicker skin, a mouth with hideous hamburger meat gum tissue, and enough teeth to chew through an entire city.

The gaping-mouth monster swam into the victims who were battering against the oppressive tides of water and gathered them up. The shark had eleven people thrashing in its mouth at once. Most were impaled on teeth, half-chewed, gored, or missing limbs.

All were bloody.

All were soon to be dead.

The shark had twenty people in its mouth cavity, then thirty people, and then fifty people before it closed its mouth and chewed the thick wad up with a sickening crunching of bone and the sound of guts bursting through skin.

The beast swallowed them whole.

One GULP, and all gone.

Ram knew that could be him next.

Swallowed.

Devoured.

Chewed alive.

The great white showed no signs of slowing down. Its hunger would never be satisfied. The flowing water propelled the killer onward in a flash of speed. The shark seemed to be looking into Ram's eyes and enjoying his fear. The shark bared its three-hundred odd teeth and used that new push of water to reach Buffy and him that much faster.

Fifteen yards out, Ram didn't have anywhere to go. Everywhere, enormous waves of water were incoming while other tides were bashing against him. The room where Mercy landed was overflowing with water too. Nowhere to escape, he thought, except right into the jaws of death.

Buffy wrapped her arms around him.

She too knew they were as good as dead.

Ram did his best to enjoy Buffy's embrace as the great white killer loomed nearer for the slaughter.

LEFT HANGING ON THE LINE

Ernie Pine did his best to ignore the sounds coming from outside the elevator. He knew the place was being flooded on every floor. Soon, they would all drown.

Not me. I know the way out of this mess. Fuck everybody else. I'll start the new world. My seed will carry us on. The original plan is done. There's only me now.

Ernie's body was shaking uncontrollably. He saw the president of Globo Corps gunned down by so many bullets. Bryce was dead. That made him in charge of upholding Globo Corps' vested interest. Eyes set to the future, he thought. Ernie could make decisions about Second Earth, and how the future would play out for humanity. He owned so much power.

He scratched that from his mind, knowing power was useless if you were killed. Ernie grabbed the phone next to the elevator's buttons. He dialed the security office. There was no answer.

Was the ship's security team taken out? It was very much possible. There were terrorists on their ship, as well as those terrifying shark creatures.

Ernie wasn't ready to give up.

He dialed the pilot's quarters.

Again, no answer.

The phone rang and rang.

"Damn it. Okay, think, Ernie. Who else can help you?"

Ernie dialed for the ship's maintenance crew. Ernie dialed the kitchen staff. Ernie dialed the cleaning crew's office. Nobody answered.

Everybody was eaten, or slaughtered by a religious crackpot.

That left one option remaining, and it was up to Ernie to activate that option.

The Pathfinder 3000 was the final and last resort.

Yes! The Pathfinder would get results.

Ernie dialed a series of numbers into the phone. Once he did, an automated messaged asked for voice verification.

"Ernie Pine," he said shakily. He couldn't smooth out his words. "Activate Pathfinder 3000."

The automated voice said, "*Pathfinder will be fully charged in thirty minutes. Activation will then proceed.*"

"Fucking idiots didn't charge the Pathfinder? Seriously? If the security staff is alive, I'm firing them."

Ernie knew he had to reach the topmost section of the ship. That's where he'd reach the security office, and ultimately, meet-up with Pathfinder 3000 once the special weapon was fully charged.

Ernie pushed the button for the topmost floor. He inserted a special access key into the wall and unlocked the elevator's ability to access the security quarters.

The elevator moved upwards. He was relieved to be on his way to safety. Ernie steadied his breath. Pathfinder would escort him to the safety space crafts, and he would land on Second Earth in one happy piece. There was a lot to the plan that had been ruined by this horrible turn of events. Ernie would have to make the best of things. And take advantage.

Each floor that ticked upwards, Ernie's sense of growing calm was instantly taken away from him. Small pools of water were bleeding up from the floor. He heard water splash on top of the elevator in a hard pelting rain. He imagined the elevator was under a roaring waterfall.

Ernie wedged himself into a corner when the elevator started to tremble. A small chunk of the wall broke. A mouth surrounded by hideous blue flesh bit down on his palm. A jagged one-inch bite was removed from his hand.

"*Ahgod!*"

Another hole was bashed into the floor. A bigger mouth tried to eat both of his feet, but Ernie jumped to another corner in time.

He checked the elevator panel.

Ernie was almost to the security floor.

The ceiling was being pounded by dozens of different things. He caught the steely glint of fishy eyes. Teeth crunching on metal. Wood being chewed to pulp. Ernie was soaked head to foot in shivery cold water. Something very large was pounding its head over and over against the floor.

DOOM!

DOOM!

DOOM!

The elevator dinged.

The doors sprang open.

The moment Ernie leaped forward, the floor exploded, and the head of a great white shark surged with its hungry mouth agape.

HAVE MERCY

O' heavenly father, we now present to you our weekly tithing. Mercy, you know what to do. Reach into the bag and pick something out. Really look around in there. The bag's deep. Get your hands bloody. Choose well. Sin is sticky. So sticky, it clings to you.

Dig in, Mercy. Don't be shy. Make your choice. Yes, Mercy, yes! Great selection, my boy. A severed hand! That's a very good choice.

Now place that hand in the tithing basket, son. Show the heavenly father what we do with sinners. We give them back to the maker, so he can re-make them in heaven.

Now why don't you put something else in the tithing basket? There's many other parts to choose from. Get your hands nice and bloody.

To know sin, Mercy, is to also know God's will.

Go ahead, Mercy. If it's one thing I want you to remember, my son, it's to be generous when giving to the good lord.

Our tithing baskets are always heaping with gifts to him.

* * *

Mercy flew through the door and crashed into the guest room. Ram's punch had enough force to lift him off of his feet. He landed on a bed covered in strewn guts. A woman's head was stuck between two pillows, the neck stump jagged and serrated from a serious bite from serious teeth.

God's creatures are working alongside us to bring everybody where they belong.

88

The lord provides.

I shall reap his will upon the sinners.

Water was spilling from the continually forming cracks and gaping holes in the walls. Floods were gushing from every direction. Whatever shark had killed the people in this room was long gone. He was alone here.

Mercy was slow to think. Ram's punch had both his nostrils bleeding. A bomb had detonated in his sinuses. He could taste iron leaking down his throat. He didn't have a chance to stop the bleeding. He had to go back out there and slaughter Ram Rogan, the biggest sinner of all.

Mercy was trudging against the ever-rising waters back into the hallway when a giant tide rolled towards him. He caught sight of the great white shark swim by in a blur of motion. The shark's passing caused a new ripple of water, and that ripple forced him back into the room he just exited. He was pounded by many sources at once. Mercy was hoisted up off of his feet. He was thrown right up to the ceiling. Mercy cried out in terror, afraid he was going to die before his mission was over.

He closed his eyes, and prayed, prayed, and prayed to survive this ordeal.

For the massacre was far from over.

THE 1%

Irving White was one of over two hundred elite members of Globo Corps' top investors crowded into a large convention room. *This* is the way they were being treated, Irving thought. Herded like cattle. Packed like sheep being led to the slaughter. This was second class living. Sub-standard accommodations. The room was hot, stuffy, and without food or refreshment, or even anywhere to sit. *Such treatment. Un-fucking-acceptable.*

A team of twelve security members had led Irving, and his many fellows, into what was called a "bug out" room, for safety reasons. The walls were extra thick steel. No water was going to flood into this part of the ship. No sharks, or psycho killers, or whatever else, were going to invade their space either. This was the safest part of the ship. Guaranteed. It was also the most boring part of the ship, Irving thought. Globo Corps could've at least sprung for a wet bar or threw a Rembrandt painting on the wall.

Chatter and restlessness filled the large space. The room was getting hotter, and stiflingly so, as everybody was unleashing their displeasure at how things were being handled.

And what had happened to poor Lindsey Messingham? She was enjoying her dry martini one moment, then she was screaming in absolute agony the next. Irving had seen how her fingers had sizzled off. That pink water had splashed onto her arm from that damn water fountain, and dear God, she had no arm anymore! Where had the officers taken her? Nobody would answer that question.

Everybody was demanding answers for this gross malfeasance.

The disdain was a growing humidity in the room.

Irving really wanted a drink, a cigar, and a fine set of legs. His set of legs had drowned on the fourteenth floor at one of the many open bars on the way to this box trap. Betsy Boatwright was a super model, actress, and she loved the way Irving slurped caviar from her naval. Betsy was now a dead buoy moving about the ship.

Damn Globo Corps, he thought. *The fuck ups! I paid too much money for this to happen.*

A pair of security officers stood at the head of the room and demanded everyone to be quiet. When one officer produced a knife, cut a thin track on his arm, and drew a holy cross in blood on his forehead, everybody shrank to the back of the room, including Irving.

Two others posing as security guards opened the double doors at the room together.

One of the women whose cross bled down to her mouth in heavy trails shouted, "THE LORD'S WILL REIGNS SUPREME!"

A great wall of pinkish water blasted into the room. The giant wave slammed into the hundreds standing in the room. Tidal waves smashed people dead into the walls. Tiger sharks, blue sharks, killer sharks, and many other varieties all invaded the room. Irving thrashed in the water and could see fins slice across the rising surface.

He expected to be devoured whole. What happened instead confused everybody who was still alive once the water settled. The room was five feet high with water. The sharks were forcing the hundred odd people into the center of the room by slowly tightening the circle they made around the survivors.

The boxing in was going on for several minutes before the next thing happened. From each set of gills on the sharks, a noxious pink gas exuded. Those in the room couldn't help but to breathe in the sulfur-smelling fog. And when they did inhale, those alive wished they hadn't survived.

A new grotesque reality became their living hell.

THE MOUTH OF THE BEAST

Ram had fallen onto his back. Buffy was clutching onto him and screaming in an ear-piercing shrill for her life. His back struck something that felt like a cross between leather and fruit skin. Teeth large enough to chew up a bus surrounded him.

They were inside the great white's mouth!

Ram wasn't sure how he got it in his hands, but there it was. A steel rod. Maybe a damaged part of the ship, he guessed. However it happened, he thanked God for that rod, because he was using it to keep the great white from biting down on them. The rod was wedged on the top of its tongue and up against the roof of its mouth.

The great white shark roared with anger. Buffy kept unleashing her terror. Ram kept his arms firmly on the rod. If that mouth bit down on them, they were finished.

The evidence of certain death came from the screams echoing from down its cavernous throat. Dozens of people were lamenting their terror in the dark. They could hear stomach acids reduce bodies to digestible liquids. Pops, gargles, belches, stenches, and screams played on repeat.

Ram couldn't think beyond the simple fact of being trapped in a shark's mouth with only a steel rod preventing them from being eaten alive.

How could they escape the shark's mouth?

The shark beat its head against the wall. It was trying to shake them out of its mouth. Ram clung to the steel, and Buffy latched onto his body.

The shark launched itself full-speed down a hallway stretch and slammed into a wall. Ram was knocked backwards, struck the top of his head against the back of a tooth. He let go of the rod, but Buffy quickly clutched onto it. The problem, she wasn't strong enough to keep it wedged in place. She was too scared to do anything. Ram could read it on her face, that strangled look about her.

The collision not only knocked Ram forward, it also forced up a broth of partially eaten hands, torsos, and ravaged bodies from the shark's throat. Sickening as it was, Ram was grateful, because a .50 caliber M-60 floated in that gruel mix. It was covered in strings of pearly white guts. Ram didn't care. He grabbed it and started firing at the roof of the shark's mouth.

"Die you fucking *shaaaaaaaaaaark!*"

Bullets blasted mouth debris in every direction. Shards of bone, bullet casings, jets of syrupy blood, and hot brain paste were chewed up and turned out. Soon, the shark stopped moving altogether.

Ram couldn't believe it.

He had blown a nice hole through the shark's skull.

The machine gun was out of bullets. Ram threw it aside, helped Buffy off of the tongue, and they used cracked sections of skull as the purchase to climb free out the top of its head.

They were now in a different section of *The Redeemer*.

Up ahead was a courtyard full of blooming flowers and trees. It was the nature walk corridor. Floods of water had turned the area into an upside down mud pit. The glass walls were streaked in mud, blood, and fish guts.

Ram noticed most of the bodies in this area were lower ranking security officers. Many had their throats torn out. Eyes were vacant holes staring into horrible death. Other bodies had suffered bites from smaller sets of teeth.

"I don't understand," Ram said. "This doesn't make any sense."

Ram didn't realize how bad they looked until he had a good look at Buffy. Buffy's hair was caked in a red gelatin mess. Chunks of shark brains were glued to her clothing. She looked like she'd crawled out of some nebulous monster's gut cavity.

Buffy was pissed.

"What doesn't make sense, Ram? The world being burned up? A super space ship flying us to safety? A guy with a cross painted on his head wanting us dead? Mega sharks attacking us on a space ship? What *specifically* doesn't make sense? Please, fill me in. What else does this day have for me that'll stump my brain?"

Ram couldn't lose her to the insanity of the situation.

"Get yourself together! I know you're a strong woman. Don't prove me wrong. I need your help. Look at these bodies. They weren't attacked by sharks. The wounds are too small. So what killed them?"

"I don't know. You want me to call the police?"

"Buffy, please!"

"We're not making it out of this alive. If you expected a polite end of the world buddy, you picked the wrong fucking bitch."

"Listen. You hear that?"

The ceiling of the courtyard started to tremble. Squares of wood paneling started to come undone. The structure was giving out to the pressure of incoming water. The entrance doors, already off the hinges, allowed the new tide of incoming water to rush in at them that much faster.

"Run!"

Ram shoved Buffy forward. They were stomping through thick mud. Their pace wasn't fast enough, and in seconds, massive waves knocked them to the ground. The room was overflowing with raging, angry walls of water.

He was plunged under the surface without power to resist the tide's force. The water was doing its best to drown him. He had lost Buffy. He wondered if he would ever get her back.

Whatever was turning the ship inside out would easily snuff him dead. He kept trying to reach the surface and couldn't find it. Everything was growing darker as his lungs tightened. Pinpricks of painful sensation attacked his skull. He was going to drown; that much was certain. Ram was sure the same fate would befall Buffy.

One good thing would come out of this ordeal, Ram thought. At least he wouldn't be eaten alive by a shark.

NO MORE MERCY

The congregation at the Church of the Holy Salvation watched the Super Bowl game in rapt attention. Mercy was also engaged with the big screen in the main area of their church. The pews were packed to full capacity with their fellow members. The St. Louis Rams were winning by two touchdowns. Half-time was drawing near. Mercy could feel the tension rising in the room. Then that tension broke when Jake Lazar appeared in the end zone. The camera panned in close. Jake threw off his black shroud and revealed the bricks of C-4 covering his torso. They heard Jake's practiced sermon over the television.

"I am the Red Revolution. God has willed it, so it shall be. We know of Globo Corps and the future of the world, and how mankind will end. Choose death now. Go willingly to God. I am the hand of G—!"

Mercy choked on his shock.

The congregation gasped.

Others were crying.

The camera panned to quarterback Ram Rogan sending a Hail Mary from mid-field. The football sailed high and then punched Jake right in the nose. Jake fell into the end zone, and landed on his back with blood burbling from his nostrils.

Mercy's brother didn't get up.

It turned out he wasn't unconscious.

Jake was dead.

Ram Rogan had subverted the will of God. Such incredulousness! How dare one man go up against the will of God? Mercy vowed in that moment the bastard would pay for this injustice. Mercy came up with a plan to enact such a measure, and shared it with his grief-stricken congregation.

Mercy reached out with his hands, grabbed hold of the broken chunks of wood, climbed, and thrust his body upwards through the gaping hole in the ceiling and avoided certain drowning. The water that surrounded him in that guest room had lifted him to safety. The guest room below him was completely submerged in water.

God is watching out for you.

He wants you to complete his task.

Mercy realized he now was in another guest room. He wasn't alone. A familiar face shared the room with him. Her name was Sharon Hillman. She was a younger member of his congregation. Sharon was twenty-one years old. Mercy remembered how Sharon dated his brother before his death. She wanted to carry on Jake's legacy.

Sharon was sitting on the floor. She had a gaping bite-wound on her side. Her midsection was leaking blood very fast. She wasn't going to be alive much longer.

Mercy lowered to her level and held her close.

"You are a worthy vessel of God, Sharon. You have done the Red Revolution proud. Jake is watching over us, and he knows you did your very best."

Sharon wasn't accepting of his words. Her face was a strange mask of contempt. "I have seen things nobody should see. The things that did this to me, they're hideous. Just, hideous! God can't exist in a world that's bred such evil!"

"You mean the sharks did this to you?"

Sharon's words were laden with the blood quickly filling up her mouth. "No, Mercy. Not the sharks. Something else. Something very evil. Hideous.

"God is not watching over us. God left us when we launched into space with these awful sinners. Just kill me. I can't stand it. The things I've seen. *They can't be un-seen!*"

Mercy picked up the machete that dangled loosely in Sharon's hands.

"God loves you," Mercy whispered. "You will be with him very soon. Say hello to my brother. Tell him I'll be there soon with him, up there in heaven."

Mercy dragged the machete's exacting blade across her throat.

He listened to her choke and gargle on blood. Sharon's face reflected relief. Almost a degree of joy, Mercy thought, as she edged closer and closer to death. She could see the other side, and she liked what was incoming.

When Sharon's corpse went limp, a new energy surged in Mercy's veins. The Red Revolution wasn't over. Not even close. People still lived and breathed on this space rig. One thing he vowed to do before his own death: confirm Ram Rogan was dead.

The football player had taken so much from Mercy, and his congregation.

God willed it.

So shall it be.

Mercy stormed out of the guest room with machete in hand and the hunger for death gleaming from his eyes.

TIGHT QUARTERS

Death was cold. Death was a dark confining space. Death was a blow to the skull. Death was a paralyzing feeling of fatigue. Every inch of Ram felt like death. His muscles ached from top to bottom. He had blood flowing from the top of his head. He had struck something on the crown of his skull that created a small gash. The pain from the wound was the thing that convinced him he wasn't dead. He was very much alive, and very confused.

The tight space resembled a coffin. He couldn't twist around, or stick out his arms or legs. He was squished between four walls of confining steel.

Ram tried to piece it together, now that he knew for a fact he wasn't a goner. He had been fighting those incoming waves inside the nature walk area. He must've been forced up to the ceiling. Yes, he thought, because he had struck his head on a torn part of the ceiling, and that metal was sharp. The next time the waves shot him upwards, there was an open duct, and he reached for it. He must've hit his head again and blanked out.

Lucky, Ram thought, that he managed to get inside the duct system before going unconscious. If he'd fallen back into water, he would've drowned.

This situation wasn't exactly something to celebrate. He could only inch forward. Each shift, he was rubbing the skin on his elbows and knees raw. Ram couldn't turn around. He could only worm forward.

Worst yet, Buffy was missing.

Ram called out to her until his voice gave out. She could be down in that nature walk eaten, drowned, or a floating piece of shark bait. Ram tried to turn around in the tight duct space. The feat was impossible for his bulk.

He called out to Buffy some more, with the same results.

She was gone.

Ram decided he wasn't going to find anybody stuck in this tight space. He crawled forward, using the limited energy he had left to fight his way onward. His knees were bleeding. His elbows were stinging from broken skin. Ram clenched his teeth and kept fighting to move. There had to be a way out of this duct, he kept thinking. The space felt like it was getting tighter and tighter. He imagined being in a giant's closed fist, and slowly, the giant was clenching that fist and waiting for him to break.

I'm not going to break, Ram kept telling himself. *I won't. Damn it all, I won't!*

He kept crawling onwards, bumping his head and back against the top, and doing everything his body could do to muster forward.

Was he heading in a direction of escape, or was he going deeper into an unknown dark abyss? What if he hit a wall and couldn't turn around? He would die here. Maybe he would've preferred being eaten alive. Horrible as it would be to be chomped into pieces, at least it was fatal and quick. Dying in this tight tomb would take days. Agonizing days.

Panic filled his body. Maybe he would break after all. His heart was beating a thousand pumps a minute. The metal walls seemed to hug him. Ram sucked in air, and all he got back was his own stale, burning hot breath. It felt like there was a plastic sack over his head, the way the air was fruitless and so thin. The energy in his body was depleted. This was as close to being dead without actually being dead, he thought.

Ram stopped where he was, and gave a deep gasp of defeat.

I can't keep going. I'm going to die here.

I should've burned to death on Earth. Why was I allowed to survive this much longer, if only to die like this?

That dooming question kept repeating in his mind.

What broke the cycle was the sound of rushing water. He felt a cold chill brush across his burning hot body. When the great wave of water struck him, Ram was a clog in a pipe that was about to be dislodged. The force of the water propelled him forward. He couldn't move, thrash, or fight the event. Ram was drowning in the powerful rush. He was a streak of increasing speed. Wherever the water was going to take him, he wouldn't have long before he drowned.

SHOW NO MERCY

Mercy clutched the fish wire sticking out from in-between the dead woman's legs. He stood before his congregation ready to continue with the proceedings. Mercy tugged back on the string and made it taught, but he did not pull backwards on it. Soon, he thought, would be the time for that special part of the ceremony.

"The woman who lays on this alter," Mercy announced to his congregation, "is named Amber Larken. Her flesh, her body, her blood, her vessel, is the holiest of the holy. She is a lost descendent of Mary Magdalene. Her body is the closet to God we can get without actually crossing over to heaven. Being re-born in this womb shall bring your young ones closer to God. They will grow with love in their hearts, and the lord's blood upon their bodies."

Mercy pulled back on the fish wire. Out came two of the infant's feet, tied together by the wire. The wailing baby was covered in Mary Magdalene/Amber's blood.

Mercy raised the baby in his hands, prayed to the infant, and then returned the baby to his parents who were weeping in joy.

The next set of parents in line approached Mercy with their baby.

He tied the string around the infant's feet, and shoved the crying child through dead Amber's widened gash for a vagina, for the child to be reborn through the holy womb.

Mercy stared down the blade of his machete. The surface was a gory mudslide of pink gobs of tissue, half an eyeball, a severed toe, and a partial cherry of an intestine. How many had he relieved of their lives and sent to their maker for judgment?

Not enough. People still lived and breathed on this ship. They should've burned on Earth, and now, Mercy was the one who was going to make things right.

He was stalking through a restaurant whose tables had been swept up in a great current of water. Dead bodies lay like dying bloated husks on the floor. Mercy poked them with his foot to ensure they were dead and not just unconscious.

Mercy searched through the backroom kitchen to find a bloodbath. The cooks were dead. His followers must've seen to their deaths.

He searched the freezer and fridge and didn't find a soul. He did happen upon hundreds of thousands of dollars worth of smashed wine and spirits. The storage room was all broken glass. Someone was buried under that glass. The man was nothing but exposed skin. A glass porcupine.

"Serves you right, *sinner*," Mercy said. "You should've been praying for your soul instead of wetting your whistle. Now we'll see which master you'll be serving on the other side."

Mercy was disturbed from his search by a condemning voice. And for once, it wasn't a voice in his head.

"You're not fit to judge those around you. That's a job for God. You are obviously not God."

Mercy spotted the man standing across the kitchen. He was on the other side of a giant hole in the floor. The mystery man was hunched over and clutching his side. This man was injured, and the pain was evident in his voice. He was dressed in black from top to bottom with a white collar. He kept his face turned, so Mercy couldn't see his features.

"I am closer to God than many," Mercy argued. "I am not God. But I represent his wishes."

"Oh, do you?" The man was amused. "I thought that of myself once. I would lead the survivors to Second Earth and keep the word of God alive. I'm the ship's Chaplin. I delivered some award winning sermons when *The Redeemer* took off. I had non-believers eating out of my hands, and the believers, they were weeping idiots falling over in the pews. It's the kind of sermon that made me think I was God's mouthpiece. That God was channeling himself through me. It's all a lie. A damn lie."

"God is the word," Mercy growled. "You're supposed to be reverent."

"I know what I'm supposed to be! But what I've seen, it contradicts God. It contradicts everything!"

The man pivoted his body, so Mercy could see every detail of his face. Half of his features were normal. Nothing alarming there. He was a preacher in his sixties with bold white hair. But God in heaven! The other half of his face was soft skin melted down into waxberry trails. His mouth and eye slits were stretched back several inches. Along his neck, and down to his chest, were deep slits that resembled shark gills. The man was breathing through them, visibly and audibly. His inhales and exhales sounded like sick rheumy whistles.

Mercy wasn't ready for the grotesque sight. "What happened to you? Why are you—?"

"Why am I hideous, you mean? If you would've seen the others out there, you'd think I was beautiful. You haven't seen ugly, Mercy Lazar. Yeah, I know who you are. You're one of those crackpot religious terrorists from Missouri. You bring shame to the word of God. Judging by how your machete gleams red, you've been murdering the survivors on board. You're nothing but a cold-blood lunatic.

"Maybe nothing matters anymore, huh? God? Space? Second Earth? It's all doomed. I don't know what I am anymore. Human? Shark? Monstrosity? Who knows? But I do know one thing, and that's how I want to swim in water. I want to tear the flesh from my prey. I want to crack bones under the power of my jaws. I want to hunt, kill, and *de-vour!*"

Mercy threw the machete at the shark-thing that threatened him. The machete stuck him in the ribs. The man hobbled back three steps, leaned against the side of an oven, pried the weapon from his torso, and laughed in a sickening shrill.

"You'll have to do better than that, Mercy!"

The Chaplin bucked forward and winced in pain. "It's happening again! Oh, you'll see! *Ah-hah-hah-hah-hah-hah-ha-haaaaaaaaa!*"

Mercy was searching the kitchen for another weapon to finish off this cackling madman when out from between the Chaplin's flesh-gills exuded a pink gas. The gas sprayed with a sharp hissing sound. The pink haze obscured the room in five seconds. That gave little time for Mercy to escape. He backed up from the cloud, but he'd already taken in several breaths.

The gas stung his nostrils. It made his mouth tingle painfully and water to the point he was drooling constantly. His lungs expanded in his chest. It felt like fiberglass was cutting up his lung tissue. He buckled onto the floor and coughed. Soon, he was hacking up blood.

No matter what he did, Mercy couldn't remove that wrong feeling that was penetrating his body.

"It's about time you were judged, Mercy," the Chaplin laughed. "Look in the mirror when you're transformed, and then we'll see how you feel about the word of God. *God's a funny joke we all love to tell!*"

Mercy barely saw it through the pink haze, but he certainly heard it.

Through the huge hole in the floor, the head of the great white shark came forth and snatched the Chaplin's body. The incredible jaw power! It crunched him into three pieces before gulping him down loud enough Mercy could feel the concussions of breaking bones rattle the floor.

The shark fell back into the hole.

Mercy could only cough, and then shriek in pain as his body began to metamorphose.

UNBELIEVABLE!

Ram was a flaccid, helpless thing caught up in a surge of water pressure. Forward he kept moving. He was struggling to fight the urge to breathe. Soon, he would certainly take in water, aspirate, and die. Die anyway, he considered. There was only death in this trap.

Ram closed his eyes tight, heard the water bash against his body, endured his sides banging against the walls of the duct system, and hoped there would be an end to this assault.

There was a loud POP sound. Metal crunched. He opened his eyes to catch the ducts ahead of him had come undone from the great water pressure. He was headed straight for that opening. Ram pointed his arms ahead of him, turned his body right, and angled out of the duct. He crashed down from a ceiling and hit the ground with a thud.

Ram rolled, then stopped. He lay there exhausted, breathing hard, and trying to make sense of the turn of events. Water was flooding from that hole in the ceiling. Then the flow ended. Whatever stroke of luck he'd received, that luck had quickly turned sour.

Once the water stopped, from out of the ceiling raged a bull shark. He had seconds to react. Ram wouldn't be able to run and escape. The bull shark was coming right at him. It had torn the sides of the duct system, the shark was so huge. Its sides bled from the process, the fishy flesh hanging in shreds. The bull shark's face was twisted in rage as it bore down on Ram's location.

He leaped up to his feet, leaned forward, put his shoulder into it, and bashed that shoulder into the bull shark's belly. The collision knocked them both in two different directions. Ram flipped twice, struck the wall, and landed on a soggy mattress strewn in the hallway.

When his dizzy head cleared, he was on his feet again and ready to take off running when he saw something very strange. The bull shark was on the ground writhing, bending its body, and choking on something. This was going on for minutes until the shark gave one more cough, and out it spit a human body. That body crashed through its clenched teeth, shattering them into porcelain pieces.

That body was Buffy.

Ram ran to her. She was a wadded up thing cast to the ground. He cradled her in his arms. She was covered in a red gelatin sheath, but Buffy was otherwise unharmed. Ram used the four inches of water pooling in the hallway to wash her body as clean as possible.

Buffy finally opened her eyes, saw that it was Ram, and hugged him close.

Words spilled out of her. "I was trapped in a duct, and then all I could hear was metal tearing, and then I was swallowed up, and I heard screams, and people were grabbing me, but they weren't alive, they were really pieces of people bashing against my body, and I knew I was dead, but then I open my eyes, and I see you, Ram, and thank God for you!"

Ram let her cry for a minute. She had survived a terrible ordeal. Ram took that time to scan the hallways. This area was very different than the rest of the ship he'd seen. The floors were solid concrete. The ceilings had lights inside of wire cages. This area was behind the scenes. Security clearance only.

Ram helped Buffy to her feet. She was still shaky and weak. Ram gave her that extra support, and they walked against the water in the room that was knee-deep. They moved carefully past the bull shark with agony on its dead face.

"Where are we going?" Buffy asked. "You act like you know where you're going."

"Listen."

Ram put his finger to his lips. Buffy trained her ear to any sound. Beyond the trickling of water, a voice could be heard.

The voice of Ernie Pine.

CATCHING UP

Ernie Pine was two lefts and a right from their position. Ram kept his ears keen to the evil bastard's voice. Ernie wasn't talking to any one person. He was talking to a machine. The device on the wall resembled an ATM. Ernie had both palms pressed on a screen, and he kept saying his name.

"Ernie Pine. My name is Ernie Pine! Let me in! Goddamn you, what's your malfunction? Ernie. Pine. Ernie Pine! ERNIE PINE! Ah, fuck you."

Beside the ATM-like device was a solid steel door marked SECURITY. As he guided Buffy towards Ernie, Ram wondered what the SECURITY room really entailed.

Ernie heard them tromping in the ankle-deep water and turned his head. He looked like a guy caught masturbating over a sink. "Ram? Buffy? You two made it."

"No thanks to you or your crew," Ram growled. "Now I want some explanations. Why are their sharks on this spaceship? And don't act like I don't know about your little plan with that bald weasel to kill me once we reached Second Earth."

Ernie jaw dropped. "I'm very sorry, okay? Everything's different now. I won't lie. Everything you say is true. But Bryce Saxon, and all the big shots from Globo Corp are dead, or about to be dead. I don't know why there's a bunch of sharks on this ship. I swear it."

"You lie through your teeth. Maybe it's about time I start busting some of those teeth, and maybe by the time you're all gums, some truth will slip out of your face. How about that idea?"

Ram grabbed Ernie by the front of his suit and threw him up against the wall. He cocked his fist back. Depending on what came out of Ernie's mouth, he might or might not bring five fingers across Ernie's mouth.

Ernie talked fast.

"Everything's gone to shit, Ram. Absolutely everything. I had nothing to do with what's happening. I saw those religious extremists—you know, the Red Revolution crackpots—carve up I don't know how many of our guests. They snuck onto the ship through the cargo hold. I got the report from the engine control room shortly before they too were attacked. They flooded the ship to keep us from being melted by that pink shit."

"Yeah, and what about the sharks? Did Red Revolution bring those on board as well? Last time I knew, terrorists don't use sharks to do their dirty work."

"Well, these extremists do." Ernie was exasperated. The man was limp in Ram's grip. "Actually, that's not true. Before Globo Corps believed the earth was going to set itself on fire and wipe out humanity, the company pumped hundreds of gallons of water from several coasts to fill *The Redeemer*. When the water mixes with our fuel, it turns into energy that allows our engines to run."

"Yeah, yeah, yeah," Ram spat. "I don't need a lesson about your special space ship. I saw the video. Why are there sharks on this shit ship?"

Ernie's eyes stayed on Ram's cocked fist. "When they pumped that water from the ocean, the sharks survived the process. They've been marinating in that pink liquid. They didn't melt. They survived. And they're mutated and very hungry. They're eating everybody in sight. It'll be us next if I don't get into this security room."

"What's inside?"

"Besides four walls and a roof," Ernie quipped, "you've got the only thing that might save us."

Buffy asked, "And what's that?"

Ernie's eyes blazed with confidence.

"The Pathfinder 3000."

ENTRY

"I can't tell you what the Pathfinder 3000 is," Ernie quickly explained. "I have to show you. The only way to show is if we can get inside this room. The security panel won't accept my handprint identification."

Ernie pressed his palms against the flat screen.

"See? Access denied."

Buffy swiped Ernie's handkerchief from his front pocket and wiped the screen dry. "Maybe if the screen wasn't wet, that would help."

"Yeah right. We'll see about that."

Ernie tried his hands again.

Access granted.

The security door unlocked itself. When Ernie Pine opened it, from both ends of the hallway, they heard water rushing in towards them. Great tides of it were splashing in their direction. Sections of the walls burst open. The ceiling imploded and added to the speed of the tide.

"Get in NOW!" Ram urged Ernie and Buffy ahead through the door. "No time!"

Right when the powerful wall was about to sandwich them from each direction, Ram forced the door shut. Water clapped together outside and spread out with a strange fizzy noise. When the water settled, they heard multiple bodies sluice through the waters outside. Fins cut through liquid. Ram swore it sounded like sharks swarming around a piece of bloody meat.

Close call, Ram thought. Too close for his taste.

He studied the room they were in, and was surprised at the large size. There were muted red lights shining from single bulbs. The walls were bare concrete. Ram was surprised water wasn't getting into the security room.

Ernie seemed to read his mind.

"This room is sealed air-tight. We have limited air supply that's not connected to the outside of this room. We are secure...for now."

Ram noticed Buffy leaning up against the wall. Her eyes were globes of terror. She was visibly shivering. Her hands hugged her body tight. Buffy's nails were digging into her skin and drawing cherry beads of blood.

"What's with her?" Ernie asked. "We're safe. There's no reason to turn into a flake."

"Shut the fuck up, you asshole. Don't talk for a second."

Ram put his hands on her arms and spoke softly. "What's wrong?"

Buffy's voice was soft at first, and then it hardened into something sharp and icy. "Before we came in her, *they* were out there. In the water, I mean."

Ernie laughed. "Sharks? Yeah. Obviously. Great observation, lady."

"Shut up, Ernie. I swear I'll break your spine. Let her talk. What did you see, Buffy?"

"They were hideous, nasty things. I just want to erase it from my mind. They were horrible. I still feel nauseous thinking about. Ram, they were beyond scary."

Before Ernie or Ram could ask what she had seen in the hallway, a new voice spoke from the other end of the room.

"What she saw was science fiction fantasy made real. Her reaction is perfectly normal. Fear is something you better get accustomed to on *The Redeemer*. This is no longer a fun space ship for the rich crème-de-la crème. This is a horror show. Everything on this ship either wants to devour us, or gut us for God. Terrifying as it is, if we're going to reach the emergency ships located in the bowels of the ship, we need our wits and our spines."

Ram scanned the room. Beyond the walls lined with storage lockers was a fenced in square with numerous shelves stocked with things he couldn't see from his vantage point. What Ram could see was the man in a plain button up shirt and army fatigue pants. His gray hair was put back in a long ponytail. It took a moment for Ram to recognize this man who had a strip of grenades strapped across his shoulder and chest.

This was the man from the introduction video to *The Redeemer*.

Dr. Dean Fleming.

The scientist spoke with a confidence that stole everybody's attention.

"I have something to show you in the back room. Once you understand what we're up against, then, and only then, can we start worrying about how we're getting out of this death box alive. I can't guarantee all of us will make it. Depending on how hard you listen to me, you just might increase your chances of survival."

Dr. Fleming turned, and headed to the back of the room. "Follow me, please. I know this has been a trying time. But you have to stay strong."

"Let's check it out," Ram said. "I want to know what this egghead has to say."

Everybody followed the scientist into the back of the room.

ALARMING DISCOVERY

Dr. Fleming did most of the talking, while Ram, Buffy, and Ernie did the listening.

The lockers in the middle of the room were marked with a strip of white tape. On the tape were the names of various persons drawn in with magic marker. The one that struck Ram the most was the name "Shrapnel". Buffy was about to ask where these people were, when Dr. Fleming cut her off.

"They're all dead. Died right when the flood gates opened. There's lower level security goons, and then there was these guys, who were supposed to be the hardest of the hardcore. They died outright. What a waste of personnel."

Ram was more interested in the fenced-in square at the other side of the lockers, and the tall casket-like box that was all tinted black glass. The gated square had tarps covering the walls. Ram could see indentions beneath, but he couldn't figure out what was being covered.

"We'll get to all that stuff later," Dr. Fleming said, following Ram's eyes. "First, I have to show you what I know. The more we know, the easier it'll be to fight back against those things out there. Because we're going to have to if we ever dream of getting off of *The Redeemer* alive."

They were near the back of the security room. This was a break room. There were beer cans on the sink, stubbed out cigarettes in ashtrays, and half empty bottles of hard liquor strewn on the floor.

"Globo Corps was confident our special security team wouldn't be necessary. There were lower ranking security who escorted you off of those ships who delivered you to *The Redeemer* before it launched, and these officers were designed to take out the serious life-threatening problems. If they occurred."

Ram scoffed. "You mean the type of threats with teeth and Bibles? Those kinds of threats?"

Dr. Fleming appeared to be ashamed of how things were handled on the ship.

"Yes, exactly. Those idiots were liquored up, overconfident, and not prepared to save anybody's life. They got themselves, and just about everybody else, on the ship killed. Who knows how many people are alive at this moment? Very few, my best guess. A better guess, it's just us now."

"Why did you bring us back here?" Ernie jabbed his finger in the doctor's direction. "You don't have to rub it in, Dr. Fleming. I know things went to shit, and it's Globo Corps' fault. I get that. Our company fucked this up. This was handled incorrectly. So what? What the fuck does it mean now? It's too late to take it back. You can't bring people back to life. Globo Corps can't do everything. Some things even money can't fix. Now let's move on. Please."

Dr. Fleming seized Ernie's pointer finger and twisted it backwards. "I get some things too, Mr. Pine. I know what you were planning to do with certain people on this ship before we landed on Second Earth. You sick son-of-a-bitch."

Ram stood next to the doctor. "I know for a fact he was going to kill me when we arrived there. Your friend, what's his ass, Bryce Saxon, was going to have me accidentally die. All because I'm Samoan. You guys planning a master race on the new planet? Should I call you Hitler, Mein Fuhrer?"

Ernie was pouring sweat and blubbering for his life. Tears and mucous downgraded the power-suited man into a diaper-filling baby.

"I'll tell you everything. Don't kill me. I'm so sorry. Please. You can't understand it unless you're on the inside of it. When you're talking about wrangling billions and billions of dollars from various persons, some people get to make decisions. Whether you agree with them or not, it doesn't matter. I wanted a seat on this ship. I wanted to ensure *The Redeemer* could fly us off of Earth and get us to a new and safe planet.

"The people at the top of Globo Corps wanted to improve our population. We're talking about having sixty-percent white, twenty-percent black, ten percent Latino, and ten percent other. Globo Corps had a guest list on this ship, and some were going to be allowed to have children, while others wouldn't. Those who wouldn't would have to be sterilized. Same with jobs, and roles in the new community. We needed a certain number of hard laborers, teachers, engineers, doctors, survivalists, scientists, you name it. It was all planned, and the guest list reflected that.

"What we didn't count on was the ferocity of which the earth burned. Many people didn't make it. But Globo Corps was willing to work with that, because we have some people already living on Second Earth. We'll be okay."

Dr. Fleming slapped Ernie across the face so hard that he tumbled to the ground with a sharp cry.

"You're leaving out the juicier tidbits of the story. One tidbit in particular. Tell it all, Ernie, or I swear, I'll break your neck right now and call it a day. I can take my chances with a pretty lady and a football hero just fine."

"Okay, okay," Ernie cried so much he was coughing. "Certain people would be killed when reaching the planet. It takes a lot to get *The Redeemer* in the air. You got crew working in the engine room. You got cooks, kitchen help, hospitality service, people cleaning your dirty laundry, and party hosts, and so many people who aren't on the list to make it to Second Earth. They were going to be taken care of once they reached the planet. I don't know how. Something humane, like food poisoning."

Ram growled, "Food poisoning is humane to you?"

"Look, I don't know how they were going to be killed. There's people on Second Earth who are representing Globo Corps' interest who deal with these kinds of tasks. They would do the killing, so-to-speak."

Dr. Fleming snarled. "They would do the cold-blooded murdering, you mean?"

"Yes, yes. Everything you say is correct."

Dr. Fleming breathed in and out to calm himself. "I worked for Globo Corps for decades, so I could visit Second Earth, and see its potential, and save lives. I was naive. This wasn't about saving humanity. It was about Globo Corps claiming humanity for their own interests. Just like America liberating Iraq. They only wanted their oil. Humanitarian efforts and big government don't mix."

An automated voice spoke on the intercom:

TWO HOURS UNTIL SELF-DESTRUCT MODE IS INITIATED. THOSE ON BOARD REPORT TO FLOOR ZERO FOR SAFETY PROTOCOL.

Dr. Fleming snapped out of his soap box moment. "We don't have time for this. I'm going to show you this real quick, and then we're going to get moving."

He reached for the table where a towel covered up a lump. Dr. Fleming removed the towel and revealed a baby lemon shark. Dr. Fleming had used a steak knife to slice open its torso down the middle.

"Very quick, you see the organs have been modified. You get larger large intestine and bigger small intestines. The heart has grown to twice its normal size. New teeth, stronger jaws, and an insatiable hunger for blood and meat have compelled these sharks to do anything and everything for food. I see dozens of digestive sacks. They're designed to eat and eat non-stop They'll never be satisfied. There are other new components I can only guess as to what their function is. One thing that troubles me is the thickness of their skin. It has quadrupled in thickness. I had such a hard time cutting this thing open to poke around."

Dr. Fleming then explained the process by which Globo Corps pumped water out of the oceans and how the marine life got mixed in. Then he veered right into the true cause of the shark attacks.

"When I visited Second Earth, I studied local plant and animal life. It's just like earth. It's a chip off the old rock. But with one big difference. Oil.

"Instead of black Texas tea, when we took soil samples and accidentally struck pay dirt, out burbled this pink crude. The oil on this planet is very different. The creatures who lived and died on this planet during the age of dinosaurs must've been something beyond imagination. We haven't had the time to dig deep and search for fossils yet. That was supposed to come later on. But we got plenty of this pink stuff. It's an amazing substance. It burns clean.

"It turns out, Hydrolyne, as I call it, can fuel an engine a hundred times better than black oil. Globo Corps and their team of engineers were able to build an engine based on perpetual motion. You mix Hydrolyne with water, and keep both moving, and it acts like a super fuel. That's how we were able to build a super ship to take so many people off of Earth. The project was rushed, because the company's scientific team believed Earth was going to terminate itself any day now.

"Those sharks trapped in our engine were immersed in that pink stuff. Whatever capabilities the pink stuff owns, it's changed those sharks into the ultimate killing machines. They can survive out of water. They have the strength to move about without the aid of water, and they can move like bullets. It's clear they're dangerous. So we need to arm ourselves if we're going to get into one of those emergency ships on Floor Zero."

Ram's interest piqued. "What kind of weapons are we talking about here?"

Dr. Fleming's smile was a jackal's.

"Space weapons."

ARM YOURSELVES

Dr. Fleming threw the towel back over the baby lemon shark and guided them towards the fenced-in square. He opened the main door that was padlocked, and each of them entered. Dr. Fleming removed the tarp covering the main wall. A steel rack displayed an odd array of futuristic weapons. Each gun was similarly built. Ram imagined laser tag meets steel and polished blue barrels. Others had cylinders that carried ammo versus traditional clips. The biggest difference between the varieties of weapons were the colors. They were neon yellow, neon blue, neon red, and neon white.

"These look like little kid guns," Ram joked. "What do these weapons do exactly?"

"I just want off of this ship," Buffy said. "I want to breathe in fresh air and walk on grass. I'm tired of being surrounded by steel. Give me what you got, and let's get moving."

"We'll get you off of this ship," Dr. Fleming reassured her. "As long as you're willing to fight. You have to listen to my instructions. These guns do way more than fire a bullet. Most of them don't even fire bullets. That's why our top-notch security force didn't use them. They only wanted conventional weapons. They were macho hot heads. I say that was very stupid on their part."

"Just tell us what they do," Ernie insisted. "We're running out of time. That bitch over the intercom said we have two hours before this ship blows itself up. You point and shoot. How complicated can it be?"

Dr. Fleming checked himself. Ram could tell the scientist's patience was wearing thin. "I'm only going over this once. Each gun has a unique ability."

Ram listened as Dr. Fleming went over the gun's capabilities. The yellow handled guns were called "Displacers". They could take a living thing's molecular structure and rearrange it with gory results. "Pressurizers" exerted thousands of pounds of force on any one object and could crush and squash the enemy with alarming power. "Brights" sent a bright whitish-purple beam like a camera's flash in the direction and could fry the target with extreme heat. "Dehydrators" could remove every ounce of fluid from a target in five milliseconds. The others the doctor mentioned, he spoke in such a hurried manner, Ram couldn't keep track.

Put the gun in my hand, Ram kept thinking, and I'll do the rest.

Ram was worried about Buffy. She was exhausted, as were they all, but she had a certain emotional fatigue that could either work in her favor or stop her where she stood. He vowed to watch over her and get her safely off of this ship.

His eye was also on Ernie. The man's face was unreadable. His eyes were puffy from a long cry, but the man's inner thoughts remained elusive. Did he agree with Globo Corps' plans to kill innocent people, or was he a helpless cog in the machine? Would this greasy glad-handing schmuck remedy his mistakes?

Ram didn't know. Too much was happening too fast. There were so many threats; Ernie Pine would have to be dealt with later. If they made it to Second Earth, he would make Ernie answer for his crimes, because they were crimes, and if they were re-starting humanity, cold-blood murderers couldn't be allowed to slip through the cracks.

He had to do one thing before everybody chose their weapons. Ram grabbed Ernie by his tie and pushed him against a locker. Ernie closed his eyes tight, anticipating a punch.

"If you're ever going to live alongside good honest people, Ernie, you're going to have to prove yourself. Now's the humble beginning. You try anything, you'll never redeem yourself. You get how important the coming hours are to your future?"

Ernie's eyes popped open. "Yes, of course. I can apologize all day long, and it won't mean anything. I couldn't change things. Globo Corps is too big for me to do anything but obey their orders, no matter how criminal they are. The company turned into a monster, and I did too. I was helpless to stop it. I have to live with the blood of many on my hands. I only want to get off of this ship, save who I can, and if I'm lucky, start over."

It sounded genuine, but Ram still had his reservations.

Ram let Ernie go.

Everybody selected their special weapons.

He urged Buffy aside from Ernie and Dr. Fleming, who were both talking animatedly about something.

"I got your back. You know that, don't you?"

Buffy gave him the best smile she could. "I know you do."

Ram kissed her cheek. "You need to start believing it. We're going to make it. I'll stake my washed-up reputation on it."

That made her laugh.

Ram dug into his pocket. "I snagged a pack of cigarettes and a lighter from that break room. Why don't you have one?"

Buffy accepted the offer, and they were both smoking.

"You can talk all day about how you're going to save me, but smoking this makes me feel a lot better."

Ram enjoyed his smoke. "Look, if we make it, I'll promise you this. If we become an item when we reach Second Earth, you can eat, drink, smoke, and do whatever the fuck you want. That much I can promise. You're your own woman."

"You got yourself a deal, handsome."

Ernie and Dr. Fleming approached Ram and Buffy. Ernie guided them back into the fenced in box and had them stop in front of the tinted black casket that was propped on a steel platform. Ram imagined the casket to be a giant phone sitting on a charger.

"Now here's the ace up our sleeves," Ernie bragged. "Call this a down payment on a real apology. Things went to shit so fast, we didn't get a chance to use it earlier. It could've saved lives. But I guess we're far from being out of the shit just yet."

"And what is this down payment exactly?" Ram asked. "Another space weapon of the future? Maybe a Globo Corps brand douche?"

"No," Dr. Fleming said seriously. "Not a douche."

"Then what is it?"

Dr. Fleming's fingers dialed a series of numbers on a small panel on the front of the glass casket. There was a great air hiss of decompression. The front opened on a hinge. It wasn't until the series of blue and red lights blinked on that Ram could see what was inside, and Dr. Fleming announced, "*This is the Pathfinder 3000.*"

PATHFINDER 3000

Dr. Fleming couldn't hold back the awe and reverence of his creation.

"Now that he's fully charged up, we can use our special friend here. I'm talking about some serious ass kicking. I created this cyborg war machine from the body parts, organs, and brain tissues of eight soldiers killed in the line of duty. Only the best. The very cream of the killing crop. Surgery, transplants, nitrous power, super concentrated battery power, and the finest of cutting edge weaponry stands before you. Pathfinder is your best bet, people, if you want to keep your asses alive.

"Imagine the leanest tissues, the healthiest of organs, the vitality of youth, the cunning of a spy, and the deadly exacting precision of stone cold killing machinery. I'm talking peak performance. Space age technology and cybernetics. Pathfinder 3000 is two parts cryogenically sustained human flesh, and three parts metal, anti-freeze, and ballistics and weapons. Pathfinder is a walking battalion of kick ass. The enemy destroyed, guaranteed!

"It's designed to protect the innocent. That means us, people. It'll find anybody in trouble, locate them, and take out any threats from between here and Floor Zero. With this guy, we're going to survive this."

Ram was startled when Buffy clutched onto him. She was startled by the ripped two-hundred pound super soldier who stepped out of the glass casket. Ram imagined Duke from G.I. Joe. An action figure with a testosterone upgrade. The machine's cheeks were sucked in so hard Ram could see the indentations of his teeth. Its steel was painted deceptively like human skin. Its back bulged along the spine as if the cyborg had a giant battery stored there. The strangest thing was its giant fists for hands.

Pathfinder's voice was also discomforting. It sounded like a wholesome father talking about the birds and the bees to his son. Very much Ward Cleaver from *Leave it to Beaver*.

"You are safe with me, folks. I hear you've had a few scares tonight. Let me put those concerns to rest. Anything that threatens your lives, I will crush, kill, and destroy it. No exceptions."

Buffy gasped when Pathfinder stepped towards them. Each time the machine planted its foot, it sounded like a stomp. The thing had to weight a ton, literally.

The cyborg stood in front of Ram. "Hold still. I must scan you."

"Scan me? Huh? Wait a second. What?"

"Let him do it," Dr. Fleming said. "If the laser is disrupted, it could blind you."

"Sweet Jesus! Blind me?"

Ram didn't move at all. He held his breath. He prayed the sweat running down the side of his head wouldn't be a distraction for the cyborg.

He was shocked when the cyborg extended his pointer finger an inch from his right eyeball. Pathfinder's fingernail lifted from the tip. A red laser was produced under the nail and scanned his eye.

"No threat. His only intention is to reach Second Earth and impregnate his female friend."

"Thanks, dick," Ram complained, once the laser finger wasn't pointed at his eyeball. "Man code, Pathfinder. Don't tell everybody *all* of my secrets."

Buffy didn't react. She already had the laser finger on her eye. After five seconds, Pathfinder gave his verbal assessment.

"No threat."

"That's all?" Ram was angry. "You didn't scan any secrets in there you'd like to share?"

Dr. Fleming intervened. "He's still got a few bugs to work out. He'll make mistakes as he goes."

"A few bugs?" Buffy reacted once she too didn't have the laser in her eye. "He's fully loaded, right? He's got a tank inside him, and you're saying he could make mistakes?"

"He's all we got," Dr. Fleming argued. "Think. Just us against what's out there, forget it. We'll be dead. Pathfinder is the closest thing you're going to get to evening the odds."

Pathfinder 3000 was scanning Ernie. Ernie's face had drained into the color of cheesecloth.

Pathfinder 3000's verbal assessment came quickly. "Strong threat to the innocent."

The cyborg's hand clutched Ernie's throat with a vice's grip.

"*Gaaaaaak!*"

"What is it doing?" Buffy gasped. "You can't just kill him."

Dr. Fleming stared at what was happening with a respectful silence.

Ram was about to charge the machine when Pathfinder 3000 spoke.

"Ernie Pine plans to use you to get to Second Earth. He has friends there who will help him kill you all. You each pose an imminent threat in this man's mind. You, Ram, because you'll ruin the gene pool. You, Buffy, because you're not safe. You don't agree with Globo Corps' future plan for humanity. You wish to expose their wrongs. You'll throw the community into upheaval. You, Dr. Fleming, won't survive either, because Globo Corps has a team of younger scientists on Second Earth who fit Globo Corps' mold better. This crew doesn't ask questions. They just obey orders.

"Globo Corps was planning on retiring you once you stepped foot on the new planet. Ernie Pine knows each of you will reveal the secrets you've learned on this ship to the community who know nothing about the company's wrongdoings. Therefore to protect you, Mr. Pine must die."

Ernie was thrashing to escape Pathfinder's chokehold. He gasped, choked, and bent his body to slip free, and the man ultimately failed. Ernie's face changed from red to a deep purple before he stopped thrashing and died. Pathfinder dropped him on the floor with a hollow thud.

"Wait," Ram said. "Why would Globo Corps make a machine like this? I mean, if it can see through to your thoughts, wouldn't that be like suicide? I mean Globo Corps' full of evil, right? They'd be asking for it."

"Globo Corps approved my project," Dr. Fleming replied, "but they didn't approve the way I built this machine. I had a feeling when we reached Second Earth, I might be in danger. This bad boy is my insurance policy. I designed him with special features, against orders."

Buffy eyed the doctor with distrust. "Then why don't you let your friend scan you? We all did it."

Dr. Fleming walked up to the machine. "Scan me, Pathfinder."

Pathfinder did so.

"No threat."

"How do we know you didn't program it to say that? How can we trust anything this machine does? You work for Globo Corps. What makes you so different than the rest of the assholes who work for them?"

Dr. Fleming agreed with their concerns.

"I'd be thinking the same things you are right now. I came into this operation, because I knew Earth was going to hit the self-destruct button any day. We had no other options. I had to do what I had to do to save humanity. I also knew if I survived and made it to that planet, me and my machine could make a difference and take on Globo Corps. I could make a difference."

The doctor cleared his throat and stuck out his chest. "And if that speech isn't convincing enough, then there's one factoid that'll make you believe me."

"And that would be?" Ram asked.

"If I wanted you dead, you'd be like Ernie already. *A corpse on the floor.*"

PART SIX: FIGHT TO FLOOR ZERO

MERCY

Mercy was crouched in the corner of a semi-dark room. The only light was from two oil burning lamps. Mercy had slept on his sleeping bag on the hard floor. Everything was covered in a layer of dust. He was sticky from top to bottom with ancient cobwebs. He had stayed underneath the secret room in the Church of the Holy Salvation, what would later become the Church of the Red Revolution. He was only ten years old now, and didn't know what to do with himself. The lanky child stared at the shadows and tried to understand his purpose here.

What was he supposed to be seeing down here in this box? Or maybe it wasn't something to be seen, but instead, to be heard?

He trained his ears harder.

He heard absolutely nothing.

He had seen absolutely nothing.

So what now?

Mercy searched through the cardboard box for any more candy bars. All he was given were candy bars and a few bottles of water to live on. That food collection had been quickly depleted. His stomach growled. How long had he been in this dark secret room? Judging by how weak and hungry he was, far too long.

Have your vision, *his father told him,* and when you have it, knock on the door. I'll let you out. Then we'll talk. You're about to become a man of God, my boy.

Mercy cried remembering what his father had told him because Jake, his brother, had seen many things in this secret room. They had a strong bond together. Mercy felt like he had nothing to offer the cause. He was a useless member to the family, and worst of all, he was useless to God.

He tried harder. His eyes bored holes through the walls. Mercy shouted in anger, because he was failing. He balled up his fists, punched the floor, and cried until he fell asleep. When he woke again, Mercy remembered one thing his father told him in the case he didn't have a vision.

He would finally try that suggestion.

He held out little hope of it working, but still, he had to try.

Mercy got up from the floor and walked to the head of the room. He stopped in front of the rocking chair, then sat in Grandpa Lee's lap.

The child asked the withered skeleton dressed in preacher's clothing for advice on how to have a vision.

Nothing happened.

Mercy kept looking deeper and deeper into those deep chasms for eye sockets. He put his hands carefully into the bared hands of a skeleton for comfort. Mercy hoped for answers. Anything.

He felt foolish.

This was a waste of time.

He would have to knock on the door and tell his father he had failed.

Before Mercy moved to do just that, the bone face turned down to Mercy, and out from the withered stinking throat, Grandpa Lee gave the boy the answers he needed.

Mercy enjoyed his new abilities. He could slice across the water faster than any of the sharks that stalked the floors for fresh meat to chew. He could smell flesh and blood. He was so hungry.

Where had everybody gone?

Was everybody dead?

No.

He smelled the living. They were out there.

Mercy arced his body, swam with the tide of flood waters down what used to be the giant escalator, and reached a security officer limping across the main foyer with a wooden baton in his hand.

The security officer cried seeing Mercy's hideous form come in for the kill. "You're hideous! Kill me then. Just get it over with, you ugly son-of-a-bitch!"

Before the officer could shout another obscenity, Mercy grabbed the man by the head and legs and forced his body to bend the wrong way. Mercy tore him in two like a sheet. Mercy gobbled the organs and meat that spilled from the victim's gaping open body. The warmth, the thickness of the meat, the way his teeth could liquidate even the toughest of flesh and gristle, the meal only further anointed Mercy's hunger.

Mercy stalked through the guest corridors, recreation rooms, open bars, the fine dining restaurant, and searched for more bodies to consume.

He sensed others like him, among the sharks and sea life, and knew he had competition. They were all so very hungry. Every predator could smell those who remained alive on the ship. There were very few alive. He vowed to be the one to eat them.

Every last one of them.

LEAVING SAFETY

Dr. Fleming loaded everybody up with shoulder holsters that carried four of the laser tag space guns. Two guns hung on each side of them. The doctor also gave them a metal compass that was electronic. It would tell them where to go via an automated voice in order to reach Floor Zero.

"In case any of us die on the way down," Dr. Fleming said, "I don't want to leave any of you helpless. Once you find the emergency crafts, you step in front of it, the door will automatically open, and the system will do the rest."

"You mean it'll take us to Second Earth without a pilot?" Buffy asked.

"Exactly."

Ram couldn't take his eyes off of Pathfinder. The man/cyborg looked on awaiting the doctor's next command. "So what if exits are blocked, or we can't access the elevators or stairs to get to Floor Zero?"

"Then we make our own way," Dr. Fleming said. "Our friend here will take care of that."

Pathfinder 3000 clenched his fist. "I will keep you alive, as long as you stick with me. No cute stuff, Mr. Rogan. I don't play games like you do. I don't score touchdowns. I score blood."

"What the hell? Does this robot know who I am?"

"Pathfinder's a walking information system," Dr. Fleming said. "He knows everything about us. I hope to use him as a kind of library to show the future generations born on Second Earth how things used to be."

"When do we kick some ass?" Pathfinder said in his robotic monotone. "I'm ready whenever the rest of you are done gabbing.

When it comes time to fight, I hope you won't wimp out on me. You either make 'em bleed, or you're bleeding out your vagina. And sharks love the smell of blood. If you're bleeding, it's tampon time. Raise your hand if you don't have any. I'll provide the feminine napkins."

"Huh?" Buffy laughed hysterically. "I love him. He's full of bullshit."

"Just don't forget I'm human," Ram said. "I'm not programmed to be funny. I just am."

"Jealous of a machine?"

Dr. Fleming stepped between them. "We need to get moving. Time's ticking."

Pathfinder moved towards the main entry door. "We stick together. Stay close. Nobody goes off on their own. Don't make me look for you. If you take me away from obliterating the enemy, I won't be happy at all. I take the lead. Talk only when I ask you a question. Understand?"

Everybody said they understood, except for Ram.

Dr. Fleming nudged Ram with his elbow. "Tell our friend you understand. He won't move until you agree to the terms."

"O-kay. I agree. But why do I have to tell him that?"

"No questions," Pathfinder said. "It's a verbal contract you just made with me. Now let's move. No talking back, or I shoot you myself."

Is that supposed to be robot humor? Ram thought. *Things keep getting stranger by the minute.*

Pathfinder pressed a series of buttons on the wall console. The door opened. Everybody tensed up. Water leaked into the room. Seconds later, they were ankle deep in it. A severed hand floated by them, alongside wads of bloody and torn up clothing.

The cyborg moved ahead of them. Its head turned in a complete circle, its eyes sending out a laser and scanning the area.

"Clear."

When the four exited the Security room, they left Ernie Pine's body behind.

Ram, Dr. Fleming, and Buffy stayed tight together. Pathfinder moved three feet ahead of them. They could only hear their own footsteps tromping in the water. They kept on for ten minutes and arrived at the emergency stairs.

"Stay put," Pathfinder instructed. "Scan emergency stairs. Threat detected."

The door shot open so hard, it flew off the hinges. Pathfinder was thrown across the hallway. Out came a long octopus tentacle. The hand clasped around Buffy's midsection and lifted her up in the air. Ram aimed his gun, but he couldn't get a clear shot. The tentacle was shaking her up and down like a can of soda. Dr. Fleming's expression of terror proved he too didn't know what to do either.

"Drop the lady!!!"

Pathfinder rocketed towards the tentacle. Flames shot out of his feet. The machine was a streak of speed. His right hand turned inside out, and out unfolded a spinning metal saw blade. The blade sliced through the tentacle, freeing Buffy.

Buffy crashed to the floor, splashing down.

Ram charged through the open door, down the staircase, and spotted the giant octopus climbing up to the top floor towards them. The thing was the size of a yacht. He unloaded four frantic shots from the yellow gun.

Bright green laser beams pounded home. The smell of burning metal and the rotten egg smell of sulfur filled the area. The octopus turned a bright green color. Its body seemed to tremble, and in two seconds, the thing dried out and shriveled into a rotten black husk a third of its original size.

"Way to avoid getting your balls wasted," Pathfinder quipped. "Hell'uva weapon you got there. Thanks for not pissing your pants. Don't let the compliment go to your head, All-American. Shit's only going to get worse. You haven't proved anything to me, tough guy. This isn't football. This is war."

"The fuck is with this machine? Is he going to insult me the whole time? Why doesn't he pick on somebody else? I haven't done anything to you. We don't have a prior relationship. So why me?"

Buffy couldn't help but smile. "What? You can't take a few jabs, All-American?"

Pathfinder was already stalking down the stairs.

Buffy and Ram had to double their speed to catch up.

The stench wafting from the dehydrated octopus was like smelling wet dog food rotting in the hot humid summer heat. The octopus was still sizzling as they stepped over the lengths of charred mess.

Down three new flights, nothing else happened. Along each staircase, water was steadily falling. Ram thought of waterfalls, and calm, and not being eaten.

Ahead, the length of staircase below them was chewed up to the point it was impassable.

"Enter this level," Pathfinder instructed, pointing at the door nearby. "We try the elevator when we find it. If the elevator doesn't work, we'll have to shoot the floor and climb down to the lower level and try the stairs again."

The level they entered led to a convention center. There wasn't much left of what it originally was, because they were now knee deep in water, and dodging broken, chewed up tables, fancy chairs, and bloated body parts.

A banner floated in the wide open space reading: GLOBO CORPS WELCOMES YOU. EYES SET TO THE FUTURE.

Food floated in the water. Caviar, seafood, steaks, and high end eats were rendered inedible, having mixed with human remains and tainted water.

"This must've been where the bigwigs hung out," Ram said. "They probably eat and shit gold."

"They do not shit gold," Pathfinder said. "Not another word. Keep listening."

Everybody had their weapons trained at the wide open room. Pathfinder was moving straight for the double door access. They almost made it when the doors shot open.

What they saw had them gasping in shock.

Ram had to really look at the monstrosity and turn over the details again and again. The flesh was a road map of the grotesque. He imagined a crude shark made out of the human body. That malleable clay was a disgusting lump of broken bones, twisted muscle tissue, and spread thin flesh. Mercy Lazar had his eyes and mouth stretched backwards into narrow triangles. He no longer had hair. His body was a crude shark's. His arms had been twisted back, half broken, and turned into two fucked up shark fins. The legs were wrapped up in flesh and pressed together to create a rough back fin. Gills, what looked like jagged lacerations of pink gummy skin, lined Mercy's neck and chest. Half his body was in the water and swimming towards them. He raised his head so his voice could project across the room.

"This is the deal," Mercy called out, "and this is generous. I am a man of God, and God knows no cruelty."

"Look at you, you ugly piece of shit," Ram shouted. "You're ugly as a goiter!"

Pathfinder punched Ram directly in the stomach. "Silence!"

Ram hit the wet floor, and felt every bit of air in his lungs fired out of his mouth. He was brought back in the moment when a partially eaten breast bubbled up to the surface and bumped into him.

"I make no deals," Pathfinder said. "The only deal is you're dead, you fish stick!"

Mercy couldn't make any other expression besides cunning and hunger. "Then that's that. I wanted to offer you the chance to slit your own throats and die in the water, and then we'd eat you. I guess we're just going to eat you raw! Here comes blood and pain!"

Ram, and everybody else, was about to open fire on Mercy when a new rush of water shot through the double doors and completely flooded the area. The four could only brace themselves as a new fleet of threats assaulted the convention room.

War was about to break.

SHOOTING FISH IN A BARREL

The convention room became an insane wave pool of terror. Ram lost track of everybody. He had hold of a red space gun, and his other arm paddled against the hard-hitting current. When the surge of water calmed, and he was belly deep in water, Ram could see what horrors had entered the room.

Hundreds of shark men and women were on the attack. The disfigured fish were ravenous. Jaws clacked at the water, as their gills spit out spurt after spurt of water. Their bodies moved like a school of fish, paddling fast, and charging in for the kill.

Ram unloaded four shots from a red gun. The blasts unleashed a brilliant blue laser beam. It pounded a woman whose breasts were serrated gills. Her eyes were fully exposed in the sockets, giving her an insane expression. The beam absorbed into her skin and turned her inside out, ripping flesh and exposing her insides.

"Molecular displacement," Dr. Fleming said, paddling towards Ram. "Works every time. Now watch this. This'll knock your socks off!"

Dr. Fleming clutched two green guns. "Pressurizers!"

The purple beam hit two different human sharks. It was like two giant hands clapped down on each one. They were squashed and flattened in two seconds flat.

Buffy surfaced, and she shoved a purple gun into the mouth of a man shark about to eat her from the head down to the toes. A bolt of whitish electricity blazed from the space gun. The shark's head lit up a blinding neon white color, and the shark's body twisted into itself like a wrung out towel. Blood, guts, and bile spurted from both ends.

"Fuck yeah," Ram cheered. "Show them who they're fucking with. Send them to whatever hell fish go to!"

Ram wanted to immediately take his words back. A wave of a hundred human sharks were battering the water and coming for them. Their weapons were powerful, but they couldn't hit every target before the enemy closed in.

"Step back, pussies," Pathfinder said, rising up from the water. "No need to shit your pants. Keep it inside of you for now."

Pathfinder's chest opened up. Twin barrels protruded forth. The cannons unleashed thousands of rounds of ammunition. Each bullet acted like a grenade, and hundreds of shark-human hybrids were chewed up into pulped red.

"Now's the time to duck," Pathfinder said. "Close your eyes and keep your mouth closed."

Ram did what he was told. He covered himself over Buffy as she screamed at the tonnage of human gore coming their way. A warm gut tsunami lifted them off of their feet, hurled them back twenty feet, and they landed in a punchbowl of red water.

"Get up. Keep moving. Time's ticking."

Pathfinder helped them up off of their feet. Everybody was dripping with intestines and glistening with gore. Ram had to peel a human cheek from his own face.

They had no time to commiserate how nasty they were. The automated system announced: SIXTY MINUTES UNTIL CORE SHUTDOWN. SELF-DESTRUCT SEQUENCE WILL BE ACTIVATED.

"Everybody's okay," Pathfinder said. "Even you, Ram. You haven't cried once today. You're doing real good."

That robotic asshole can say whatever he wants, Ram thought. *If he gets me out of here alive along with everybody else, he can roast me until I'm cooked through good to eat.*

They stamped through the water and out of the convention room together, awaiting Pathfinder's next command.

REMAINS

There was a lot of moving without any talking. They clopped through water levels that varied, from ankle to knee high, back to hip high, and ever-changing. Many of the walls had holes punched through them. Ram imagined sharks powering through them to reach their prey. He was growing numb to the sight of a floating body part or a wad of greasy innards spread out on the water's surface.

They cut through a room to avoid the massive waterfall blocking the hallway ahead of them. There were tables and computers left in disarray. A banner on the wall read: INTERNET USAGE. TWENTY-FIVE DOLLARS A MINUTE.

"Twenty-five dollars a minute!" Ram gasped. "Sweet Jesus."

"Wait, didn't the Internet stop existing?" Buffy asked.

"Globo Corps created their own version of the Internet," Dr. Fleming said. "It was meant to be a temporary replacement. It's really old content saved to a database. It keeps people calm when they've lost everything. Anything familiar is comforting."

Ram shook his head at the sight of a partially eaten hand clutching onto a computer mouse. "What's wrong with people?"

Pathfinder stopped and grabbed Ram by the shoulder. "I know you're a football star, and you're used to getting your way, but right now is the time to shut the fuck up, Mr. Rogan. As smart as your social commentary is."

The cyborg patted him hard on the back.

Buffy held back her laughter by putting both her hands to her face.

Fuck you, robot. Later, I'll make sure they turn you to the scrap material they use to make dildos. You'll be up somebody's ass in no time.

They kept treading in the direction of Floor Zero. There were more parts of the ship he hadn't seen. An art gallery was completely ruined. Sculptures and paintings floated in the knee-high water matched with the pieces of the patrons who had been enjoying them.

An odd smell carried in the air. It must've been coming from up ahead, Ram thought, because the stench kept getting stronger and stronger with each new step. They were inside of a health spa with various steam saunas, a Turkish bath, and a large tanning salon. Inside one of the tanning booths, a dog shark was pinned between a functioning tanning salon. It's skin was burned black and was still cooking. The shark had long since died, but the reek of burned skin was too much to take.

"Let's keep moving," Pathfinder suggested in his monotone. "You guys look like you're going to puke. I don't smell anything."

Asshole, Ram thought. He looked at Buffy. She had turned a concerning shade of green. After taking a long trek through many hallways so destroyed and turned inside out they had no idea what the areas used to be, they came upon something very familiar.

IT'S SAFE HERE

A preacher waved them through the threshold and into the church. Behind the preacher were long rows of pews. At the head of the room, a stage had a podium and a life-size statue of Jesus hanging on the cross. Other survivors were scattered about the pews. Ram counted twenty-three persons total. Everybody was wet, exhausted, and judging by their faces, checking and re-checking their sanities.

The preacher was named Christopher Bark, or as the young man of the cloth said to everybody, "Call me Chris."

"We can't stay here," Pathfinder said. "Haven't you been listening to the announcements? This ship will self-destruct in less than an hour. I can take you to Floor Zero to the emergency ships. We can make it out alive."

Chris's youthful features turned into something mean.

"We're not leaving this ship. Everybody here wants to turn themselves over to God. What we've seen recently, we don't want any more time alive. We are ready to die. The lord can take us any time now."

Dr. Fleming tried to talk sense into the shaken preacher.

"We can get you to Second Earth. You're upset right now. We're all stressed. That's understandable. Let us help you. We can make it to safety. Please, we're here to see you out of this situation alive and well. Let us help."

Chris shook his head. "Our time is up. Humanity should've burned along with Earth."

"That's right," a voice said at the door. "It's about time they understood the truth."

Mercy was half in the water, and half sticking up on the surface. He floated in place, and said, "The lord's message has reached these people. They are smart. God will be merciful. I'll eat you fast. The pain will be worth waking up on the other side and walking through the gates of heaven. I'll show you the way."

Pathfinder 3000 pointed his arm out straight. His hand unhinged at the wrist. The nub of his arm was a large gun barrel. "This barrel is like my dick. It's a long piece of hot steel about to be lodged up your tight fishy ass!"

A giant BOOM exploded. The area around Mercy was flying water and flames. Ram couldn't tell if Mercy had avoided the gun's wrath, or not.

Too much else was going on.

The survivors in the pews, including Chris, rushed to their seats and prayed. Ram's eyes widened when at the head of the room, a blue shark bashed through the wall and shattered the statue of Jesus dying on the cross. The same shark rammed through four rows of pews to get his mouth around a cowering woman and her daughter.

Ram unleashed three shots from his laser gun. The four bull sharks weaving their way towards him lit up like a CAT scan picture and were instantly cooked into flying ash pieces.

Buffy unloaded three laser shots. The molecular displacer forced the shark's guts from inside its body. Fountains of compressed innards shot out from its mouth and anus.

"God take me now!" Chris shouted. "We're ready to see you in heaven!"

Mercy lunged out of the water, snatched off the preacher's head in his mouth, and flopped back into the water. The preacher's headless body kept his hands together, somehow still praying. Two other sharks chomped on the rest of him, and the man of the cloth was nothing more than blood on the water.

Pathfinder's eyeballs were machine gun nozzles that erupted in machine gun spray. The shots scattered the fifteen circling sharks from their position.

"Broil, boil, fry, season, and fuck you up!"

Pathfinder bent forward and out his legs came large branching flames. He flew across the air with the speed of a missile. The cyborg punched through the sharks like a bullet, killing each one he pulverized.

When the cyborg touched back down, and the room was clear of threats, the machine said, "Fish are like semen. They all swim upstream."

"What?" Ram was confused. Why was the cyborg such a wise-cracking asshole? "Why do you keep saying weird shit?"

Dr. Fleming smiled. "I programmed him to be like that. I thought some humor could get us out of a tough situation. I guess I was a tad overzealous."

"It's weird," Ram said, "but at least he's saving our asses."

They weren't sure what direction to go in until at the head of the room, an entire school of sharks inside the mounting wave were heading right for them.

Dr. Fleming pointed at the hole created by the shark behind the podium. "Up there! Hurry!"

Together, the group retreated to the hole. Sharks were right behind them. Pathfinder was at the back of the group. The cyborg's legs kept taking him forward, as his torso spun at the hip, and he was turned completely around. Guns were blazing out of his eyes, chest, mouth, and arms. Between the clatter of booms and the splatter of hit targets, the group could hear the machine's maniacally-delivered quips.

"You're past due on a rectal grenade!"

"Damn shark guts stink like a Tijuana whore's tampon!"

"I never signed any petitions concerning the environment. Yeah, I'm an asshole! Fuck you!"

"Take that, you nasty salt water smelling, frowny-faced, mercury tasting, six-pack ring wearing, bait-eating motherfuckers!"

"You eat worms. You eat pawn scum. You eat each other's shit. NOW EAT LEAD!"

"Is it true? Did Led Zeppelin fuck a woman with a fish? No matter. I'm here to fuck you with my guns!"

"How do sharks mate? I guess it doesn't matter. You can't do anything with your genitals after I blow them the fuck off!"

"Die, bastard sharks!"

Behind them, gun smoke and flying obliterated shark pieces made a constant loud and wet splatter soundtrack. The narrow stairs channeled down, down, and down. The corridor abruptly ended with one big room.

Everybody halted.

What they discovered was another chamber of horrors.

EXECUTIONS

The passage behind them imploded on itself when the ceiling caved in. Stacks of broken steel pillars and shards of concrete formed an impassible hill. They were trapped in a large tiled room. The group had no choice but to stare at what lay heaped in the room.

Hundreds of corpses.

They were staff members. Those from hospitality, engineering, bartenders, hostesses, and laborers alike were pulped through with so many bullets, many were left in sloppy pieces. Bullet casings littered the tiled floors by the thousands. Holes riddled the walls. Water seeped into the room and gurgled loudly down the drains spread throughout the killing box.

Ram couldn't hold himself back. He threw Dr. Fleming up against the wall and held his fist up ready to strike the frightened man if he didn't say something that made damn good sense.

"Why is this room full of murdered people? Spit it out!"

Dr. Fleming didn't cower.

"Ram, stop! I can't say how this happened. I'm sorry about their deaths. It's wrong, and insane, and unnecessary, and plain cruel, but I had nothing to do with this. You must believe me, Ram. Please. I'm not your enemy."

Ram was grabbed by the neck and spiked onto the ground. Unfortunately for him, he landed in a pile of liquid bodies. He couldn't get back to his feet without having to touch clammy cold skin, sticky blood, and slithery cold organs.

Pathfinder stood between Ram and Dr. Fleming as a barrier.

"No more threatening the doctor. This is not Dr. Fleming's fault. According to the ship's log," the cyborg accessed his internal file, "announcements were made to each wing of the ship. They were all told to convene here for safety. They were promised safe passage off *The Redeemer*."

"And they were executed!" Ram couldn't stifle his anger, or the horror. "Murderers. It's sickening. How could this happen?"

"Globo Corps didn't want certain people to make it to Second Earth, but they needed working bodies to get *The Redeemer* up into space." Dr. Fleming crossed himself and muttered a prayer. "I'm sorry. That's all I can say. It doesn't do any damn good. I know. I'm still very sorry."

Buffy was eying the gore-drenched bodies. "In our wildest dreams, if we make it to Second Earth, you think we'll be safe there?"

Dr. Fleming threw his hands up. "I don't know. Who knows if anything's changed on the planet now that they think we're coming. It's impossible to predict what Globo Corps will do in the wake of this tragedy."

"That means it's not safe," Ram muttered. "Not now. Not ever."

"I don't know is what this means," Dr. Fleming sighed. "I haven't been in contact with those on Second Earth for months. There's honest-to-God people on that planet. They're not all like Ernie Pine and Bryce Saxon. Who knows what kind of politics are going on now? We won't know until we get there."

"Then let's get there," Ram said with a new determination. "These people can't die for nothing. Somebody has to take down Globo Corps. And if we make it there alive, that's what I'll do. The fucking scum will pay."

Dr. Fleming agreed. "I'm with you on that one. These were crimes committed. And someone will answer for them."

Buffy didn't say anything. Her eyes told him everything. She agreed with his mission, and she accepted it with conviction.

The announcement hit them all hard. SELF-DESTRUCT MODE WILL BE INITITATED IN FORTY MINUTES.

"Get behind me," Pathfinder said. "We need to keep moving."

"How are getting out of here?"

Ram's question was drowned out by the single mini-rocket that shot of the cyborg's barrel arm. The power of the blast punched through the wall. When the dust settled, a large gaping hole allowed them to sneak out of the execution room.

The group kept moving.

SHARK TACTICS

That man machine has to be stopped. Maybe I can't stop him. But I can slow them down. If The Redeemer self-destructs with everybody still on board, our plan will succeed. All will go to God. All shall be holy. As it should be.

I'll cut them off before they can leave. Their weapons are too strong for me to fight back against them. I can only try to deliver God's will.

I know what to do now.

Mercy swam hard, intending to do everything to keep Ram and his friends on the ship.

They were keeping a good pace. Ram's body ached from top to bottom. They had descended fifteen floors throughout various ruined corridors. Pathfinder kept trudging on undaunted and without fatigue. Lights were flickering from the ceilings. Some would stay lit, while others went dark.

"The ship's slowly losing power," Dr. Fleming said. "It's gradually shutting itself down. We'll be in serious trouble if we don't make it in time. When this ship blows, it'll blow to kingdom come. We'll be reduced to dust."

"Gee thanks for the update," Buffy said. "I feel uplifted."

Before anybody else talked, they stepped into a room that resembled a sandy beach that had survived a hurricane. The water beyond the fake beach was gargling and belching with giant bubbles.

Ram clutched onto his red gun. "What's next? Rabid flounders?"

"No," Pathfinder said. "Not rabid flounders. Great white shark."

Surging from the water, the great white leaped up high and landed on top of Pathfinder. The beast swallowed him whole.

Buffy kept screaming. Ram couldn't move. Dr. Fleming blinked and blinked, as if to wish it all away.

The cyborg was gone.

They expected the robot to somehow escape, but that wasn't happening. And there wasn't time to wait. The great white was coming for them next.

"Well, that's fucking disappointing." Finally Ram took charge. "Move your asses! Robo-asshole's not here to protect us anymore. I am!"

Ram unloaded four laser shots. They didn't hit home, but they displaced enough water, the great white was sucked down into a temporary undertow of spinning water.

They cut across the beach, and fled the room.

Only more horror would come their way.

This time, Ram wasn't scared.

He was fucking pissed.

ESCALATING SITUATION

Ram didn't have time to process where they were going, except for down. Dr. Fleming was ahead of them. He had laser guns blazing in both hands. A laser hit home on the belly of a tiger shark. The laser caused its innards to burst from the stomach, tie around the body, and squeeze so hard the entire mass erupted from the pressure.

"Molecular displacer!" Dr. Fleming kept shouting his war cry. "YOU LIKE IT? TAKE THAT! AND THAT! A-ND THAT!"

Buffy's guns caused everything it shot to shrivel and burn. Ten sharks were cooked into blackened crisps. Ram blasted a hammerhead and squashed it mid-air with ten tons of pressurizing force.

They were running so fast, everything was a blur of motion. They were forced to go right, then left, then double back, and bolt forward again. Somehow, they ended up on a moving escalator. They were heading down towards the ground floor.

"We're getting there," Dr. Fleming shouted. "We make a stand here and hold our own, we might just make it."

Water was breaking through every doorway. Sharks were spilling into the field of battle. They kept firing lasers and tearing up their targets until one after the other, the lasers lost their power.

"What do we do now?" Ram demanded. "Huh? I thought these were super guns. You never said anything about them running out of ammo."

Dr. Fleming touched his chest. He had a belt of grenades. He handed everybody two.

"Throw them good. Maybe it'll scare them away long enough for us to escape. Once these things go BOOM, you charge down the escalator."

Dr. Fleming pointed at the end of the escalator eight floors down from their position to a steel door that was green. The door was wide open.

"You go through that door, hurry through it, and you'll go down a short flight of stairs. That's Floor Zero. There, you'll find the emergency vehicles. Hop in, and you'll be out of here. Home free."

The automated system announced: SELF-DESTRUCT SEQUENCE WILL BE ACTIVATED IN TWENTY MINUTES.

"GRENADES!" Dr. Fleming shouted. "THROW 'EM IF YOU GOT 'EM!"

Everybody pulled the pins on their grenades and threw them up. "RUN!"

Ram and Buffy did as they were told.

The BOOMS of erupting grenades sounded like killer thunder. Pieces of fin and pink bleeding hunks rained down on them. Treading down each escalator step until they reached the part submerged in water, Ram and Buffy dove and made a break for Floor Zero.

Ram was underwater. He could hear the sound of heavy bodies strike the water. The incoming rivers were bringing in more and more sharks. He kept his eyes forward. Buffy was paddling hard ahead of him. Dr. Fleming was right behind him.

When Ram crossed through the door leading to Floor Zero, he turned around to hurry Dr. Fleming through.

Dr. Fleming was in a panic. "Hurry! It's right behind us!"

Ram saw the threat. The giant great white shark was coming at them like a thrown dart. Dr. Fleming and Buffy pulled Ram backwards and away from the doorway. The great white was a 3-D image, its head becoming larger and larger by the second. The shark slammed into the doorway. It's head was stuck between the narrow gap. The shark squirmed, gnashed its teeth, and did everything it could to come loose from the threshold.

"That was close," Ram gasped. "You see the size of that thing? It's huge!"

Buffy didn't care about the shark. "Screw it. We're here. Let's get on one of those ships and get the hell out of here. Fuck those sharks."

"You're right. Words from a scholar."

They turned around, and that's when they spotted the horrific scene. It was over and done before they could do anything to save Dr. Fleming.

The doctor's head was in Mercy's mouth. Ram could see the doctor's wild eyes and mouth unleash curse after curse. Seconds later, Dr. Fleming's head burst from the power of Mercy's clamping jaws. Dr. Fleming's headless, neck-spurting body took three awkward steps backwards and splashed down in the knee-high water.

Mercy's fluid-garbled voice seethed hatred and re-anointed hunger. "You're next, Ram. Then it's going to be that whore that goes down my throat next."

Ram clenched his fists.

"It's you and me then, Bible banger. By the time we're done, we'll see whose going to heaven, and who's going to hell."

Ram charged at Mercy.

Mercy lowered into the water and sped towards Ram.

They soon collided.

GRUDGE MATCH

Ram was all fury. He was growling like a bear, charging the human shark freak.

Mercy had the speed. It's mouth kept chomping at the water, taking practice bites. Then Mercy lunged from the water, taking to the air. Ram ducked, grabbed Mercy by the arm-fin, and forced the arm backwards until the elbow snapped. Mercy unleashed a sharp cry of pain and splashed down into the water.

Ram didn't have more than two seconds before Mercy swam at him again with the speed of a bullet. His arm fin was leaning to the side awkwardly, a broken thing. Mercy didn't take him head on. Mercy's back legs swung and pounded Ram against the back. Ram was thrown several feet and slammed into the water.

He needed a moment to remember which way was up, and which was down. His head rang like a gong struck by an aluminum baseball bat.

Mercy was already arcing his way around again and speeding towards him completely underwater.

Half the lights in the room suddenly went black. Ram had no idea where Mercy was, and that cost him. Mercy bit Ram on the arm. The man shark didn't take much meat, just a strip on his triceps muscle.

Mercy gave a stranger tittering sound of amusement.

Mercy's fucking with me. He could've killed me just then.

I need to get under his skin before he eats all of mine.

Ram clutched his bleeding arm. Mercy was poised across from him at a standstill. The shark was licking his lips and teeth in fervor.

"You know something, Mercy? The way you just laughed, it sounded like every person in the crowd when I threw that pigskin into your brother's face. When Jake fell in the end zone on his stupid ass, now that got everybody rolling!"

Mercy was all motion.

The shark threaded through the water with rage.

"I'll take pleasure in eating you raw and shitting your worthless remains out my ass! IN THE NAME OF GOD!"

"Everything you've done in your life has been out of your ass, not in the name of God!"

Ram wasn't sure how he was going to counter the shark's next advances.

Mercy pushed himself out of the water and was airborne. Any moment, the shark man would crash into him and kill him.

Ram thought fast and without true strategy.

The strangest item touched his hand.

A wet Bible.

Ram grabbed it, and pitched it at the shark. The book came open mid-air and slapped the shark across the mouth. Mercy was so confused by what struck him, Ram had his opportunity. He lowered his shoulder and speared Mercy's back. The impact caused Mercy's spine to shatter. The shark man crashed into the water. Mercy was limp and floating on the water.

"This is for my family! And this is for everybody else you slaughtered in the name of God."

Ram grabbed Mercy by the neck and the back, and putting his entire body into it, he tossed Mercy towards the great white shark trapped in the doorway.

The shark chomped down on Mercy's body and swallowed him whole.

"Cram that nasty morsel down your throat!"

Buffy treaded water to reach him. "You're bitten."

"I'll be fine. The poor doctor, not so much."

The emergency ships were very much like the hovercrafts that brought them to *The Redeemer*. When they approached the closest vehicle, the side door came open. An automated voice from inside said: *STEP INSIDE FOR IMMEDIATE SAFETY.*

The great white shark at the door applied enough force against the doorway's edges, parts of the wall came undone in big chunks. Splashing into the room, the shark slide across the water and headed right towards them.

Death was incoming.

EYES SET TO THE FUTURE

The great white was a furious man-eating machine surging across the water. Ram and Buffy hurried up the step ladder to get inside the ship. Little good that would do, Ram thought, because the shark would chew up the ship like a tin can and free up the little sardines inside.

Buffy hugged him close at the top of the stairs. "I'm sorry it's ending this way. At least I got to meet you. I almost swore off men before this."

"At least we got one last fling out of life. I guess that's all you can ask. One last good moment."

"Who knows? Second Earth might've been a shit hole."

A giant explosion erupted out the top of the great white's head. A geyser of blood and cracked skull was unleashed like a concentrated volcano. The shark crashed headfirst into the water dead.

Pathfinder climbed out the side of the shark's mouth. Half his fake skin was melted away to reveal circuitry and steel. The cyborg was battle ravaged, but still alive.

"Change your tampon, Ram, you're not dead yet. Quit slinging the English to get into her panties. You'll live to throw another touchdown. Now get on that ship and get out of here. I'll cover you. Now move out! My orders! No more spouting flowery bullshit!"

They piled inside the craft. Ram and Buffy were quick to close the door to avoid flooding the inside. When the hatch door closed, they took a look at the interior. There were several chairs, rows of control panels, a restroom, and a screen at the head of the room that came on. The giant sized screen showed a live feed of the outside of the ship.

Pathfinder's hands had become machine guns. His chest was a rocket launcher. Out his eyes shot lasers that cooked shark flesh. Hundreds of the sharks were trying to invade the port. Pathfinder was blasting, blasting, and blasting, until his body was suddenly attacked by an electrical surge. The cyborg was fried, and crashed into the water.

Dead for good.

The automated voice inside the ship announced: *Clear to take off. Self-destruct sequence three minutes from activation.*

A wall of lemon, bull, blue, and killer sharks burst through the surrounding walls of the ship's port. The aquatic attack was heading right for the emergency ship.

Buffy cried. "I knew surviving this was too good to be true."

Ram knew there wasn't a damn thing he could do to change anything. They had done everything to scrape for another moment of life.

He remembered Gaby, and the time he was standing under a burning tree outside of his apartment. A silver blanket was all that protected him from being scorched to death by acid rain. Ram was a lucky guy, he thought. He had kept to himself for the past few years. Guilt and fear had ruined his social life. He no longer played football. He didn't date. He didn't see friends. Life was better now, despite the situation. He had conquered many things post-Earth. The Church of the Red Revolution was terminated. Mercy Lazar was dead. The people who killed his wife were long gone. He made love to a beautiful woman. Ram could see himself falling in love with Buffy, if they had the chance.

"It's a shame we didn't get out of this alive. We could've kept the world going. That mouthy cyborg was right. I thought about us, and how we could repopulate the Earth. And do things right, despite Globo Corps. Someone's got to challenge the system, and keep those rich assholes at least semi-honest."

"Quit talking," Buffy said. "Kiss me before the sharks eat our asses."

Ram and Buffy accomplished the best goodbye world kiss two tired and battle weary persons could attempt.

After that, Buffy refused to watch the monitor screens. Ram couldn't keep his eyes closed. His eyes stayed glued to the head of the ship, and the multiple camera angles.

He was confused.

"Wait. A think we missed something."

"I can't watch."

"Buffy, you need to look."

They weren't in the *Redeemer* anymore. They were miles away from it. Whatever technology was used, the hovercraft's thrust and ride were both smooth and impossibly fast. The screen showed the *Redeemer* from afar. They were floating in deep black space, and the best part, Ram thought, they were in one piece.

Buffy was so happy, she laughed hysterically. "If you're not killed by religious terrorists, and if you're not eaten by the sharks, or murdered by greasy businessmen, you might enjoy a pretty view of space."

Together, they said, "Globo Corps. Eyes set to the future."

And Ram added, "*And heads way up our asses.*"

BIG BOOM

What do two people who survived near death multiple times talk about?

Ram learned the answer.

Absolutely nothing.

That wasn't by choice. Three minutes after realizing they were safe, there was a giant sonic boom. The ship was jostled hard moments later.

"What the hell was that?" Buffy cried out. "Please tell me this is over! I can't take anymore."

Ram pumped his fist. "Ye-ah! Look at the screens. Now that's what I'm talking about."

The *Redeemer* was belittled by distance. The monitors showed the giant steel hamster ball erupt. Top to bottom burst. Orange fire spread as the once space marvel was diminished into flying chunks of destruction.

"It's over," Ram said, trying to convince Buffy. "You see! The ship's gone. We fucking made it. There's no chance anything else can happen to us. We've been through fish hell, and you know what? We survived to swim another day."

"Ram, would you stop talking and *look*."

He felt his body deflate. He had to hold himself up against the wall so he wouldn't fall to the floor. "No. *It can't be*."

Thrown from the blown up space ship and picking up speed were what had to be a hundred sharks. They were champing at the air, pivoting their bodies to use the force applied to their bodies to reach their ship. Even outside the ship, the sharks craved blood, and in ninety seconds, the sharks were going to get it.

Ram and Buffy could only watch and wait for their incoming demise.

UNBELIEVABLE

Ram searched the consoles for anything they could defend themselves with. He scrambled and couldn't see anything that stood out. The system was completely automated. Designed for freaked out passengers to jump in and take a ride and nothing more.

The sharks were floating in a wall and getting closer.

"This thing has no weapons," Ram growled. "I can't make this thing move any faster. Come on, computer. Help us!"

The computer didn't respond.

Buffy was on the floor. He thought she was going to break down. What had really happened, she had located a compartment that had a silver platter of booze, cigarettes, and cigars.

"You should join me. We're dead in less than a minute. It's long enough to enjoy a few more drags and drinks."

Ram kept searching. "I refuse to give up. After everything! It can't end this way."

"It will, and there's nothing you can do about it."

Buffy was enjoying her cigarette with a smug, I don't give a fuck anymore expression. "Smoking this is better than sex. Sorry, Ram. It just is."

Ram couldn't hear what she was saying. The monitor screens said everything.

Things weren't going to end badly.

They were going to end infinitely worse.

By the time Ram decided to give up and enjoy his final moments with a sexy woman and a cigarette, the hellacious show commenced.

INCOMING!

Ram was thrown from his standing position. The emergency ship surged forward in a burst of speed. The automated voice said: *Engaging Hyper Speed Mode. Please buckle up in the safety seats for your protection.*

Ram and Buffy rushed to the seats and strapped in tight. They were posed right in front of the wall of monitor screens. The ship was weaving, turning, dropping, dodging, rising, surging, stopping, braking, and powering forward non-stop, while being jostled the entire time.

Buffy lost her stomach.

Ram lost his next.

His head ached from the constant infliction of whiplash.

He did his best to catch glimpses of the screens. There was a lot going on outside the four walls of steel that protected them. The ship's ride was a sickening one, but it was for a good reason.

The ship was doing its best to avoid the massive meteor shower!

Sharks were taking hits. The giant hunks of meteor would smash through the sharks and detonate them on impact. Some were merely decapitated, split in two, or broken into deflated carcasses. Sharks guts spread about space, floating aimlessly. Ram imagined a psychotic seafood restaurant chef's chopping block if his tools were only hammers and blunt force.

The ship kept dodging close calls with sharks and meteors alike. A shark split in two by a meteor slammed into the ship. Whatever cameras were on the outside of the ship were smeared in red. They were blind to their fate.

Ram held Buffy's hand and didn't let go.

AWAKE

Ram's return to consciousness left him full of questions.

Why weren't they floating in space anymore?

Was he dead?

Where was Buffy? Was she dead?

That question compelled him to get up and moving. He was brought right back down by the weight of his head. Crusted blood covered his face. The seat belt apparatus had snapped, and threw him from his seat. That's why he was unconscious.

Where was Buffy?

He couldn't stop thinking about her.

Ram forced himself to his feet once again. He shut his eyes against the bright sunlight filtering in through the opened side door. The door wasn't exactly open, he realized. It had been forced open.

Working his way outside, he realized the side of the ship had taken some serious damage. Meteor divots and shark blood covered the outside. Flies buzzed around the ship, tantalized by the rank smell.

The ship had landed next to a moving stream. Woods surrounded them. Ram imagined they were in a backwoods location in the Mid-west. He scanned the dense trees and down the stream. He breathed a sigh of relief when he saw Buffy bathing naked in the stream.

If there was a sight to cure every ache in his body, that would be it.

When Buffy saw him, she ran right for him. Her face was relieved. Happy tears sprang into her eyes.

"I thought you were dead! I checked your pulse. I couldn't tell if you were breathing or not. You're alive. I didn't know what I'd do alone. I thought...I thought you were dead."

"You're not getting rid of me that easily."

"Oh, Ram. We made it. This is Second Earth."

"It looks just like...*Earth*."

"A chip off the old rock. Who cares? We're alive."

She was right.

That was good enough.

For the moment.

SCOUTING FOR ANSWERS

The two of them didn't waste time. They knew Globo Corps had cities built, property sold, and people already here on Second Earth. They had to find those people.

Ram searched the emergency vehicle and found no food or water. Survival supplies were zero. After having enough time without something trying to kill them, they realized how depleted their bodies were.

Ram guided Buffy down the stream. That was the plan. Follow the stream and keep their eyes open.

The sun was blazing hot in the sky. The humidity was a sticky net slowing their progress. Deer stalked the woods. Blue birds, cardinals, robins, and a few hawks flew between trees. Squirrels were rummaging through dead piles of leaves. The wildlife didn't appear to be mutated or man-eating.

They kept a good pace for many hours. The sun was starting to go down. The backdrop was a red purple blaze. They arrived at a cliff's edge. The view went on for miles. The horizon was clear. What they saw was breathtaking.

The cityscape was tall glass skyscrapers for buildings. Buildings of the future, Ram thought, with smooth highways, cars driving without emitting fumes, and people dressed in high end clothing. They were shopping in fancy strip malls and enjoying their lives without a care in the world.

Ram saw the giant sign outside the tall gated perimeter of the city read: GLOBO CORPS. HERE IS THE FUTURE.

He took Buffy's hand and held it tight.

"You up for this?"

"What choice do we have? This is it. Literally. There's nowhere else to go. This is the future."

"The future," Ram repeated. "I guess we'll see if there's a place here for us."

Together, the two journeyed towards the city, and whatever it had to throw at them.

"Hey, Buffy."

"Yeah?"

"You still going to own up to your promise?"

"What was that?"

"If Globo Corps is out of control, we're going to take them down."

Buffy's eyes were exacting.

"Everyone of those evil fuckers will pay for what they did to those innocent people on *The Redeemer*."

Ram gave Buffy a high-five.

"Fucking a!"

EPILOGUE

Twenty miles from where Ram and Buffy's emergency ship landed, another emergency ship had touched down. When the exit door opened, the passenger immediately ran for the stream.

Fresh water! Yes. I was about to dry up in that ship. I'm built tough, but not that tough.

The shark man stayed near the bottom of the three-foot deep stream. He used his arm fins to stay in place. What he was seeing was magnificent.

Fish of many colors swam in these waters. Blue, red, and brown fish darted through the waters. He didn't want to eat them, because human flesh was much tastier. Besides, these fish were beautiful pieces of creations. He had a new appreciation for their beauty. Having come so close to dying, he cherished life. He was the last of his kind. The preservation of his species was what mattered. Mating and procreating.

That's what the sharks on the ship were doing. They were fighting extinction, just like the human passengers.

He knew Ram and Buffy were heading towards a populated area. They had survived, and so had he.

Pathfinder 3000 had let go of his neck a moment too soon. He passed out from strangulation, but he did not die. He remembered waking up in the security room alone and confused, and surrounded by sharks! The room was full of that strange pink gas. He had no choice but to breathe it in.

That was all in the past.

This was now.

Ernie Pine swam up the stream and opened up his gills and let the pink gas flow.

When he was done securing the future of his species, he would next see about getting a bite to eat.

www.ingramcontent.com/pod-product-compliance
Lightning Source LLC
Chambersburg PA
CBHW051943170626
46808CB00007B/2465